FASTEST WALK TO DEATH

New Birth through an old life

Ricardo F. Brandon

Kindle Direct Publishing

*To my siblings, my mother, my uncle George Edwards,
Rachel Stacy Spann who have been nothing but supportive,
with their love and care. I finally published it guys.*

CONTENTS

INTRODUCTION

"Why was all of this trouble on my back?" Everywhere he turned there seemed to be some new trial to discourage or defeat him. John Carter, a black young man driven to get out of the typical public squalor. With his long list of tragedies and hardship it seemed impossible to get to where he needed to go.

From losing a parent to fights his way through a racist professor, finding himself while on his journey of life on to success, and gaining one of the top positions at his law firm in Washington to facing death, and giving back. He sees the meaning in what once was meaningless.

John reveals that no matter how tough a situation may be, there will be a way.

My interest in writing came from the need to tell a story, one of hope through the face of adversity. For we all have faced it, and through these words, the hope was to claim a hand in showing the

CHAPTER 1: THE BEGINNING

A bright light shone forth; for the stage of life had been set as the first flash of the beam now hits his retina. The once dark existence, manifests into a bright appearance, never before seen, which now creates a comparison between what once was, to what now is.

Once listening through the thin walls which so vaguely gave glimpses into the unknown. For such a long time there were sounds of various causes, from familiar voices, such as a woman, whose voice brought joy, as he tried to push against his enclosed fortress. Now, the sounds of voices, and noises of beeping machinery and people busying around unfolding into fruition; the moment of unconscious understanding.

The feeling of the chilling grip of the cold dense atmosphere cascades upon his delicate skin, skin yet untainted by the world, has now broken its virgin barriers.

It is a joyful experience, but as hopeful as it may appear, the first strike brings the reality of life, as a mournful wail of the beginning of the end has commenced; only in the pain of a sorrowful cry was the joyous moment realized. The first sign of life has now been freed, which was bound in lungs which had never tasted, inhaled, or felt the touch of oxygen in the air. The journey begins.

* * *

Moments begin to fly as the sounds of now recognised wildlife truly become clear, now learning their names and their calls slowly gave way to recognition as they flowed; vibrations manifest through the blowing winds.

It was interesting to witness, the four-wheeled beasts that holds us as we travel from one place to another, revealing new things to be discovered. The slowing pull of the stopping machine, reaches the destination of where we were to be.

The soft gentle pull of a woman's hand securely grips his hand, as he steps with intention of being just like the ones he saw; he tries to put one step in front of the other as his legs shake; desperately trying to mimic the gargantuan figures, moving to and from as they towered over him.

The journey of a thousand miles has now begun.

Little to his knowledge, it would be a terrible blow again and again and it would take repeated effort and failures; though it never stopped him before. Without loss of enthusiasm, he slips once more. After he gets up an image of a soft cushion conjures within his mind; it's a white fluffy rug with its long strands like grass of yarn, covered the entire floor; but coming back to reality he came to his awareness that, that luxury was only at home.

He is in the outside world, known especially for its tough and brutish ways, hard sidewalks and noisy cares. Without loss of vigour, he is completely carefree for he has not lost the drive to walk on his own one day like the ones who tower over him. This beautiful woman with her luscious hair and bright smile is holding his hand, carefully guiding his steps and watching intently as he jerkily leans on each leg, fully secure in her ability to keep him.

Sheltered from what can truly go wrong. As he looked around he heard the blaring of a loud horn, almost deafening to the ear as it blasts with frustration, and panic. Looking back, he saw the red sixteen wheeler truck hurtling towards his direction, only four feet away. He can see the man with his blue and red trucker hat, as he vehemently waving his hands gesturing to get out the way. They stood there stunned by the fact that they were about to be hit, his frail little body, barely able to walk, braced for the impact.

CHAPTER 2: WAKE UP

Just then, Beep! Beep! Beep! His eyes opened up with shock and bewilderment, John jumped up from his soft, warm bed, as the sounds of his own deep breathes had an exaggerated intensity. He thought for a moment, as he continued hyperventilating, "it was a dream". Looking around his room that was dimly lit, he reached over to turn off the alarm clock.

There were sounds of slightly heavy knocks on his wooden door. His door was mahogany in colour, with a painting on the back of a sea captain, who was fully dressed in a Navy seal uniform; it was his brother, which he had painted himself two years ago. His brother was only nineteen when he enlisted with the seals. His name was Jesse Carter; he was about six feet tall, with wide shoulders, and thick black hair. He remembered his very calm smile, one that you couldn't miss. His presence would bring a sense of peace to the room; John missed him dearly.

Memories flooded his mind as he remembered the times they went fishing out by the sea, it was so much fun. He was his best friend, he could tell him everything, and he even missed the times they fought over silly things. Remembering the time that he took him to see his first movie, was especially fun. The cotton candy, the sweet taste as it melted in his mouth, the aroma of freshly popped popcorn. He wished he were there, but the family had not seen him for the last four years.

That's enough reminiscing as he snapped back to reality.

He forgot that there was a slowly intensifying knock on the door, it was his mother knocking. He answered with a quick "yes", for he knew too well, that any refusal to answer would mean she would just come in and pull the curtains open, as well as remove the white covering that he used when the evening chills started to creep in. As the knocking stopped he could hear her soft comforting voice saying, "it is time to get up honey", responding from the other side of the door. With a quick response he said "I'll be out in a minute".

As he realised that she had departed, he let out a sigh, still thinking about the deep impressions of the dream he just had. It seemed so real, he could feel the emotions raging through his mind. "What did it mean?" he asked himself. He had been having these recurring dreams for weeks, and nothing seemed to make them stop. The more he thought about them, the more his mind drifted into the unending abyss of confusion.

Not wanting to think about it anymore, he swung his legs over the end of his bed as his feet touched the cold floor. He jerked them back quickly off of the ground, looking down for his bedroom slippers. He was wearing his favourite robe, and he walked unenthusiastically to the bathroom to wash his face. He could hear the voice of his mother echoing from somewhere in the house. He paid her no mind, as he stepped into the bathroom.

Gazing into bathroom mirror he could see the stubble that was growing on his eighteen-year-old face, his looks were astoundingly similar to his older brother. With his jet black hair, perfectly well groomed, and his strong jawline his was a splitting image of him. He bent over as he as he turned on the faucet, and with water filling his cupped hands, he took it as he washed his face from any remainder of sleep.

Getting ready for his journey to school, he went into the shower, the cold water which quickly woke him up in the morning, made him feel better after a long night of another intense dream.

While he was showering, his mom was downstairs preparing breakfast with a determined effort that only a single mother could accomplish, to take care of her home and get ready for work.

John had not really taken into consideration all the effort that his mother had to summon on a daily basis. His father had died when he was a little boy and since then things had changed. He walked back to his room with his white towel on. Stepping into his room he looked in his closet for what he would wear that day. He decided that he would pick the red shirt today with the Chevrolet symbol on it; it was one of his favourites, because it would show his physique to the girls at school. He chose his navy blue jeans.

After, putting on his clothes he took up one of his black sneakers and placed them on. Immediately, he headed for the door where he took his watch, his bag which had his laptop, and a few notepads, which he always left right next to the dresser that was situated neatly by his bedroom door, so that he never had to look for it; if nothing else, he was a very meticulous with his things, something he admired in his brother.

John wanted to be like his brother so badly; he loved him for his deep rugged voice that rang with authority and care. Everything he did, he subconsciously had been trying to be like him, since father wasn't there anymore, and Jesse was like his new dad.

Walking downstairs to the kitchen, he went to his usual spot at the dinner table, where he took his breakfast, as he kissed his mother on the cheek, while she was washing the dishes. She was a beautiful woman with lovely burgundy hair, with lengths to the centre of her back, and very light in complexion.

She had been through so much, but like the sun that sets to allow darkness to cover half of the earth, the other side was revealed to be just as beautiful, now fully discovered. She understood the pains that life could bring, and with every moment she embraced the changing cycles of life, each season with its smiles and pains, brought greater growth like the sun after the rain. She was the epitome of a strong woman.

After John finished eating, he kissed his mother goodbye,

as he usually did just before leaving the house.

She knew that she wouldn't see him until night and so did he. She usually worked late, and he always stayed out late. So things seemed reasonably mutual.

CHAPTER 3: THE PROFESSOR

Walking out of the door he could hear the sounds of the blue birds chipping in the trees, the harmony of the wind rustling the leaves, as the wail of sirens signalled in the air, a car speeding through the street and a police vehicle trailing behind. His village wasn't the typical village with white picket fences and lemonade on Sunday afternoons. No, it was filled with women groomed in the way of manipulation and low self-esteem willing to do any and everything to get what they wanted; and the men weren't any better; ones who would do anything to make a dollar.

He lived in the slums of the city, where you do whatever it took to get to where you wanted to go. You could see the signs of abandoned buildings with broken glass, and the smell of alcohol perfuming the air, as another drunk staggers on his way home after spending another night at the bar. It reminded him of life, where the very fabrics of society fed to its people the drunkenness of vapid insignificance, while washing it down with contented mediocrity.

Dreams shattered in pieces as many drank of the poisons of neglected dreams and fear of failure; this was the epitome of this life. As all sat around the bar of choices, some drank the roughest life had to offer, while others partook of the role of being the server, but one way or another we all stood at the table of choice.

If you weren't strong you wouldn't survive a day in his life, yet he did it every day. As the cars flew past him, he remembered the day his dad died.

He remembered the sounds of the sirens just as if it was yesterday; he rarely ever lingered on the memory of those times, as it was too painful. He pulled himself together, as he put one foot in front of the other with his navy blue jeans on, and walked with his head held high in the direction of the bus terminal. He waited to catch the bus.

John sat on the seat at the bus station, and patiently waited. His mind couldn't help but wonder what it would be like to finally get out of this neighbourhood. A place where there would be no sounds of police sirens giving warnings of the distress and chaos that our community propelled to the world every day.

He sat there in silence, as his thoughts drifted into the waters of the unknown, hope aroused the excitement of a better day. Not being able to help himself, his mind danced with the dreams that came with seeing the shimmering glimpse of optimism in his opportunity of school.

He wanted to be a pilot, or a doctor, or an engineer, or a navy seal like his brother, but whatever he did, just like the men who were so determined to make money that they did whatever it took, he resolved in his mind to use that same determination to reach the top of the ladder of his own personal success.

The shrieking halt of the bus breaks as it stopped to pick him up startled him back to reality, as the bus doors swung open, the face of a very tired Mr Jenkins looked at him with a smile.

Mr Jenkins was the sweetest man that you could ever meet. He was born and raised in Southern Alabama, he was there when slavery was still a thing, but he never let that change him. Mr Jenkins' hair was fully peppered with white and black hairs as the years of aging started to display on his face, which showed the tell-tale signs of his imminent retirement.

He was a chocolate brown fellow, with his beard sprinkled

with white hairs.

He believed in the principles of manners, and he made sure he displayed it to every passenger that came on the bus.

Every morning, Mr Jenkins would start with a very polite and bright "Good Morning", but every time he stopped to pick up John, he would look at him with a half-smile and ask, the same question, with his deep southern accent "Still on the train of thought I see?" to which John would always respond, "until the horn sounded for the final stop."

They always got along.

As John stepped on the bus, he could see the rest of his school mates. There were those that were chitter chattering amongst themselves, some were laughing from a joke someone made, while the others were too busy to talk as their heads sunk deeply into their phones.

John did his usual routine and sat just behind Mr Jenkins, who had a wealth of knowledge. He was such a simple man outwardly, but deeply he was a smart and wise man. Mr Jenkins could tell the most intricate stories, with breath taking scenes, coloured with graphic descriptions, as his voice changed pitch to complement each element, literally giving his stories life.

They spoke about everything, life, relationships, it didn't matter, Mr Jenkins had taught John so much, that his maturity far exceeded the norm of his other peers. It was as though John were his own son.

John could use a father figure like that, since his brother left when he was fourteen. And knowing his dad wasn't there anymore didn't help the situation either.

It didn't matter; just being there to learn under Mr Jenkins was a pleasure. It was one of the things that added to his excitement to go to school.

It was almost like, everything that he needed to be a holistic person was copiously provided. He learnt to be better-rounded within the understanding of relationships, he got business ideas and other aspects of life, and most importantly he learnt how to be himself.

Mr Jenkins was the father he never had.

John never thought there would be anyone that he could truly relate to, other than his brother. Dad's passing really didn't impact him, but when his brother left to go to the Navy, that did.

As the breaks shrieked and the bus came to a screeching stop, John jumped to his feet and wished his father figure a good day. His feet stepped with a pace of determination and resolve to his action plan - finish school and get out of this place as quickly and by any means necessary. He would never do it the way that he saw the guys on the corner of the street did it, with underhanded dealings and dishonest compulsions.

He fixed his mind towards the goal that he would be the best at whatever he did, but at eighteen, he had not yet made up his mind. He did however have his major in the field that he thought he should pursue, and how big that field was.

He was at the University of Ohio, with its beautiful red bricked walls, peaking buildings and beautiful vegetation, filled with students.

The busyness of his counterparts moving with intentionality to their designated classes was almost strategic amongst the more studious undergraduates; and he was no better than they, as his feet sped through the enormous campus, travelling from one area to the other in pursuit of his scheduled classes.

As he walked, he could see his long-time friend Tim Cooper. Nobody knew this but Cooper was the most brilliant guy you would know, yet because of his perplexing behaviours and patterns of socializing, everyone thought of him as strange and uncoordinated, with his slender body, and pale skin.

Honestly, Tim was his best friend in the entire world, they did everything together.

"Tim," John called loudly to grab his attention. Tim looked back with a fond look of glee.

"J- Man what's up?" Tim replied,

"Did you finish the Physics questions for tomorrow?" John asked. The looks of "dumbfoundedness" and sheepish shame spurred over each other's faces. As they realised the expressions that were plastered on their faces, they laughed with enthusiasm. Bright smiles exploding from each one showcasing white pearly teeth as their gleeful sounds rang through air

John heard the sound of his black wrist watch that sounding off, beep, beep, and beep. It was the alarm he had set to signal their classes with Professor Stevens. He was very elderly, probably in his late 60s he had a partially full head of silver hair covering his scalp, which had a bald spot located directly in the centre of his head. It was the most outstanding thing that made it quite noticeable.

But also what were obvious about the professor were things only those of certain persuasions would understand.

Professor Stevens was raised during a time when, slavery had been abolished. Even though reality had changed, his way of thinking about members of the black community stayed with him. It was his obnoxious racism which permeated the air as he interacted with various students in the class.

John's paper was certainly much better than majority of his classmates, and everyone knew it, but there was a time before he started getting the grades he deserved, when Professor Stevens would insist on giving him low grades, which were undeserving.

It was the middle of the second semester when John discovered his failing grades, because he knew of his ability. He went to the Professor to inquire of his grades.

"Sir, I could not have earned these marks, I did everything that was asked, and my work was to the best." He questioned "how did I get this?" He asked with fury in his eyes and authoritative firmness in his voice.

"Someone of your background could never have written this paper." John boiled with anger as he saw his chances of leaving his retched state, going tenaciously down the toilet.

"Sir I demand to see my paper and for you to show me the basis of your markings, otherwise I will have you brought before the school board."

Professor Stevens didn't show any sign of remorse, not even an expression of disdain, it was if he didn't even exist. After this, for weeks he went to the dean of his school and through many attempts, finally got his just reward.

When he had finally gotten the grades he deserved he felt a wave of relief and satisfaction wash over him. John had made up his mind, "if those guys on the corner will do anything to make a dollar, then there is nothing I won't do to get to where I am going." This was his mantra, and he stuck by it no matter what.

Classes with the professor were many times difficult. He tried to embarrass John on more than one occasion after that, especially when it seemed he was not paying attention. It was as if he had opened a can of worms. He was humiliated by his ignorance, and he determined in his heart that every day, he would ensure that he was far ahead of his classmates, both in writing and in knowledge.

Soon after when Stevens realised his attempt to humiliate him were unsuccessful, he gave up calling on him, because it was as though the more he tried to bring him down, the more he became driven with such a fierce persistence to prove him wrong, that he excelled rather than failed.

The covered earth blanketed by the cold thick snow can be rejuvenated by the power of the hot unfolding sunlight. It was as though to say that by embracing his opposite element, he reached his mark, which would otherwise have not been revealed. A side that would carry him through life.

But today, it would carry him nowhere. Upon his entry to the classroom, he could sense a cold breeze flow through the class, as if to signify a bad ominous force.

He continued to walk as his eyes locked with Professor Stevens, who had a menacing grin. His piercing gaze, with his blue eyes hidden by years of wrinkled brought about by his elderly aged, stayed fixed upon him as he walked to his usual seat.

John knew that he did not like him, which was propelled a few months from the constant exercise of being seen before the board for his prejudice and racist mentality; but today was different, the atmosphere was so dense. He had been an A student, and never bothered anyone. It was bad enough that his family came from the outskirts of the city, where drug dealers and hookers roamed.

He lived in the stereotypical image of the blacks, the ones where murders and illicit actives seemed to be born daily. "What did I do to get this treatment" he thought for a moment. Then after a brief second he realized that it was none of his business to care, he had never been a mischievous child, well maybe at home, but he was never into things he shouldn't; well maybe a few things, nothing too bad.

Then with a sudden startling shout, Mr Carter, "answer the question!" He didn't even realize his mind had drifted out into deep thought. He wasn't aware that class had started.

"Get out of my class!"

"Sir, for what cause" he rebutted.

"Get out! Since your mind is too vacant with nothingness, to pay attention in my class."

The anger was starting to swell within his brain; he could feel emotions of rage. Every second whom passed he wanted to walk up to this bigot, and smack him into a new race. Maybe then he would be more partial to differing races other than his own.

Although everything in him wanted to confront this old man, he just took up his bag with a calmness that was so surreal it was almost scary. He had a blank indifferent face, apparently he asked about a question that was on the board, he walked up to the board and wrote an answer, as everyone watched him leave the large auditorium like room, filled with like students of all races, even the professor could see that his answer was correct.

He knew his anger came, not only because of this racist old man, but rather because he recalled the way his father died. Though He rarely ever thought about it, but seeing this old man treats him so unfairly, it caused flashbacks at the time when his dad got killed.

He too was unfairly treated, he could remember the day well, when a man the police was investigating a crime that had happened between two rival gangs in the territory, and because his description was very similar to one of the suspects, they beat him nearly to death.

Both of those officers were Caucasian, one of which had a tattoo of an eagle on his right hand. They held him down, after which one of them started to hit him. He when he finally got to speak said that he would call him lawyers and have them held for violation. It wasn't until after he went to the hospital, those things went downhill.

Their severe beating had cause internal bleeding, which persisted for days, even after he came out of the hospital dad complained of stomach pains; but it seemed like nothing at first. He said he would go to the hospital, but before he got the chance, he collapsed a few days later complaining of the same problem. He was rushed to the hospital immediately, but when he went in, he never came back out alive. It hurt him so badly because he never got to say good bye.

Every day, John made an active effort to forget, but this time it came like a load of bricks. It hurt so badly as he remembered the times his dad would pick him up. He was six years old, it was one of his favourite pass times, when he would put him on his shoulders with his favourite orange shirt that said, Team Carter, and he still had that shirt.

He could no longer allow himself to reminisce on those thoughts. He accepted that it happened, but never mourned anymore, it was as if time removed the possibility after a certain age. To go back to it was to go in a pit, which he did not want to have to climb out of again.

As he entered the hallway he could hear the footsteps of someone walking behind him, with an exaggerated pace to catch up with him.

It was Tim, "that isn't like you John", as he rested his hands on his shoulders. "You never gave up a fight so easily to that racist fool, what happened in there?"

He could look in John's eyes and see that something wasn't

right.

"I'm fine, I just really wasn't up for wasting my time today" He responded calmly.

"John how long have we known each other?"

"I don't know; it's been years."

"So are we really going to pretend as if we don't know that I know you?"

Tim had been his best friend for so long that, there was no way he could just throw caution in the wind.

John took a deep breath, as he looked over at Tim, "man you already know what it is." Tim nodded in agreement to his statement.

"Then what is there to talk about?"

Tim had no answer for his question, as John continued to walk, he turned back as said, "Please get the notes for me for later."

"Sure"

He left.

Walking out the door, he decided that he would take a walk, and what a walk it was. He started to take note of almost everything that he saw.

Walking on the road, he saw a cat that was badly bruised, probably from a fight it had before. It was mangy looking with hair that had fallen out because of the bacteria that had formed on its skin. John felt a sense of pity for this creature.

He reached into his bag, digging around for the sandwich that he had planned to eat. Since he was probably going home anyway, he thought to just give this cat piece. As it he tried to call it to him, it seemed scared and went into a corner. He could see that it had horrible experiences with humans. He walked up to it slowly, with compassion in his heart as he placed the sandwich in front of the cat.

He had never been a cat person, but something about this one was different. It looked at him with extreme caution and fear, as he pushed the meal closer, he could see it creeping forward hesitantly as it took a bite. Shaking the bread in its mouth to try to tear it from the remainder. John saw the tension of the cat slowly relax as it ate the meal.

John rose slowly as he walked away, heading in the direction to get home. He went to the bus terminal, he knew there was one person that he could talk to, and that was Mr Jenkins. As he waited he could feel something wrong in the air, a bus pulled up, but as he boarded it wasn't his father figure.

It was some strange face, this guy looked like he was in his early thirties, and he was white and had a thick moustache which sat on his top lip like a fuzzy caterpillar.

The man's face was blank with little to no expression of emotion. The drivers sometimes would give instruction if needed to passengers as they walked onto the transport, but before the man could say anything John blurted out, "who are you and where is Mr Jenkins?" he seemed almost startled at the sudden questioning. As he tensed, he responded with "I beg your pardon" with a bit of annoyance.

"Where is Mr Jenkins?" said John.

"He isn't working today; the office said that he was sick, so I am filling in for him."

"Oh," John expressed as he went to his seat quietly pondering over what it is that he should do. As the bus pulled off he couldn't help but think that he was the one person he could talk to and today he wasn't even there. Then suddenly he thought "Mr Jenkins never gets sick!"

"Sir", he shouted, "do you know what is wrong with him?! Please tell me if you do."

The man paused for a moment, and thought quietly. He spoke without even looking at John, and responded in the coldest response he had ever heard. He could feel the indifference in his voice, "He is in the hospital."

CHAPTER 4: MR CLIFFORD JENKINS

"**W**hat! Which hospital is it?"

"I really am not sure." Responded the driver

John could not fathom the thought of what could be wrong. Mr Jenkins never got sick before, in all the years he was there, he had never seen him not so much as even get a faint cough. He was the strongest man he had ever met.

Not even his brother was that strong, and he is in the navy. Nothing made sense that day. From that racist professor, to now to the man he expected above everyone else to talk to, the one who had so much wisdom.

The thought of going home really wasn't appealing, and just being in the neighbourhood, brought him anguish. As he sat there in silence, he could see his destination coming up. Pulling the cord situated just above his head, gave the conductor the signal that he was ready to make stop.

As he left, he could do nothing but think, "at least today can't get any worse." Just then a sudden shower of rain started to descend, and as the falling raindrops started to soak his clothes, he looked up at the sky and exclaimed, "of course it's raining", as he rushed for the bus terminal covering that would shelter him from the elements.

"Well, what a day" he exclaimed with a sigh, let me just get home. He waited until the rain subsided before he started walking; his house wasn't that far actually. It was so close that he could see the faded yellow and the white trim covering. It wasn't the best house in the world. The door creaked and it could do with a face lift, still, it wasn't the worst.

One thing that made the house so remarkable wasn't the archaic appeal, it really did need some repairs, but it was the memories that he had that created a deep impression in his heart; the little memories that he had of his brother or his dad was enough to make living there bearable.

Honestly, this had actually been the first time that he had been home so early in a long time. It was only 3:30 pm, as he looked down his wrist watch.

Reaching his front door, he grabbed his keys out of his pocket as he turned the doorknob to enter in. Though today had been a sincerely bad day, with class and the rain, most of all, he couldn't get Mr Jenkins out of his mind.

So he grabbed the nearest phone book to call the transportation centre that he worked for.

The phone rang twice, and then he heard the sound of a woman's voice. Her voice was soft, calm, almost seductive even, as she answered the phone, "Hello good day, Ohio Transportation Centre, how may I help you?"

"Good day, my name is John Carter, I am seeking some information. I understand that Mr Jenkins was admitted to the hospital today. Could you please help me in finding out what happened to him, and where he may be located?"

She responded with a gentle, "Sir we do not give out such information."

"Ma'am, you don't understand, he picks me up every morning to go to school, and I have never known him to get sick, ever. Please ma'am I really need to know if he is okay."

She paused for a moment, "Alright," she could hear the genuine despair in his voice. "He is in the Ohio ~~Health~~ Doctors Hospital".

"Thank you, that's about half an hour away. Have a nice day"

Before she could respond, he hung up, Click. A confused smile drew upon her face as she put the phone back on the hook.

John didn't ~~even~~ waste any time trying to find Mr Jenkins. He was calling searching through the phone book with such a tenacity it looked like a frantic monkey looking for fruits between the pages of the book.

As he spotted the number he immediately called, as he listened to the dial tone, which brought more anxiety that it did comfort.

The phone rang out, but as he hung up the phone he instantly pressed the redial button. He was determined to find out what was happening to his friend, even if it meant leaving and heading over to the hospital himself.

It wasn't like John to panic; he was trying to be calm. After many failed attempts a gentleman answered, but before the man could clearly give his generic pleasantries, John quickly interjected,

"Sir, Good day, I need to know the whereabouts of a Mr Clifford Jenkins, he is an older gentleman. He would have been admitted today, can you locate him for me, and I need to know if he is okay."

"He is in the room 203, it seems he had a minor heart attack today, and we have him stabilized."

"May I please get to speak with him?" John responded with a calm expression of relief, as he heard it was minor. Even though he wasn't fully well, he was just glad to know that he was okay.

The man merely responded "what is your relation to the patient?"

To which John answered with calm, "you could say I am his son".

With hesitation the man responded, "What is your name?"

"John Carter",

"John I don't see you on an approved list here to contact this patient, so I will have to refuse your request."

John was so mad he hung up. Determined to speak to Mr Jenkins, he didn't even wait. By that time, it was only 4:15 as he started towards the door. After leaving the house, it dawned on him then he had not even eaten. He thought for a second, and continued on the mission, he had already made up his mind.

His phone began to ring in his pocket and as he looked at the caller ID he realised it was Tim. "Bro, where are you?"

"I'm about to leave home, why?"

"You want to come over later? I have a something that I want to show you" Tim replied. Every time Tim said those words, it meant that they would do something that was either reckless or, completely experimental.

"I can't right now man, I have some things I need to do first." Tim was his best friend, but today he was more concerned with his best bus friend. He chuckled at the thought of "bus friend".

"Hey, man I'll catch you later."

"Alright J-man, call me back later."

Click.

John had a bit of a journey just to get to the hospital, and if he wanted to get there quickly before visiting hours were over, he had to make it snappy. As John looked at his watch he started speed walking for the bus that was just about to pass him, he began to flag it down frantically trying to get the driver's attention.

It was to no avail, the bus continued pass him without stopping. He could see the heads of many of the passengers turned facing the direction he wished he was going. Some with black hair, some with blond, but whatever hair they had, none turned back to give him a glimpse of hope, that is, until a little girl looked out the window to his frantic gestures.

Something must have happened, because as she saw him running like a crazed person, desperately trying to get the bus to stop, the brake lights began to flash as the bus came to a halt.

John ran towards the bus with a hurried thankfulness. He whispered under his breathe, "thank you God." He had been a young man who didn't place much notice on the divine, but still, he knew there had to be a God.

Sometimes he would sit for hours thinking - *what if there was no ultimate being governing the universe? How did it/he/she get there and where did it/he/she come from? On the other hand, if life originated through evolution, where did the matter come from to start the first bang?*

All that didn't matter now, he just wanted to get to the hospital. It didn't take them long to reach the highway. As he sat there in the bus contemplating life, a thought came to him almost seemingly from nowhere.

"What if there really is a God?"

But as quickly as the thought came into his head, it immediately was cast out, like a disposable tissue after being used to wipe one's snot covered nose. The more he kept thinking about the reality of his circumstance, and the hand he was dealt, he wondered, if there really is such a loving God in the universe, then....

He lost his concentration to the looks of a horrific crash. The vehicles had a full head on collision and it seemed as though, there could be no survivors. As a curious human being, he stared out the window at the sight of a bloody man.

His was so covered with his own blood, that his face was unrecognizable. It was clear that he was unconscious, as another man tried to drag his body from, the wreck. He could see the man ~~him~~ taking careful time to pull him out of the vehicle; but it looked futile as his body was pinned between the metal body of the vehicle.

The ambulance rushed through, alongside a truck which came with lightning speed and blaring emergency sirens. This was the second time for the day that he had heard sirens; only difference is the first was the in pursuit of man who had chosen the crooked path of life, whilst this sound came from those trying to save the life of someone that they may have the chance to be able to choose a path.

He was not that far from the hospital at this point, you

could say that he was in viewing distance. The white tower at the top with the symbol of the cross, was lit with neon lights.

It seemed that the bus was barely moving and the traffic went on forever. John began feeling more and more anxious. It seemed like the universe was intent on proving to him that things would and could always get worse.

Finally coming off the highway, John reached his destination four hours later with a sore rumpous and a dead leg, due to the traffic that was caused by the accident. It could not be a worse time. He resolved in his mind that since he came this far turning back was not an option.

He exited the bus and entered the main lobby of the hospital. There he looked directly as the nurse's station as he walked up to a very young beautiful nurse, she looked as though she were in her early twenties. She had blond hair, which was tied up in bun which gave her a very serious and mature appearance.

With her blue scrubs, she was about five feet six, with tanned skin. She gave a warm friendly smile revealing her buck teeth that were actually quite flattering. She had no remarkable features that would cause her to stand out. Her beauty was a calm aura that radiated not from her physical appearance, but rather though personality that seemed to be genuine.

For a second he almost forgot why he came. He was bewitched by this beautiful young lady.

He came back to his senses, and with a blank face, and a calm voice, he said "I'm here to see Mr Jenkins, being almost 9:00 p.m., she softly reminded him of the visiting hours, and that they were over until the morning.

It was the first time he started to get flustered after everything that happened today, "Ma'am I have travelled over four hours just to get here due to the accident, I was kicked out of my own class for a reason unknown to me, and now you're telling after all that I can't get to see the one person I look up to as like a dad."

"Ma'am, Please."

"I really am sorry I wish I could help you."

He could see she was not going to budge, it was at that point he left, at least from her view. He waited until she left, before he snuck past the front desk

He walked calmly as not to raise any suspicion amongst the doctors, keeping his head straight as if to signify that he belonged there. He knew the room number which he was going to from the phone call that he had earlier.

It was looking anxiously for room 203, as he walked down the hall, he could see the 200s and he passed each door. He had come from the other side, which meant that he would have to count downwards to the Mr Jenkin's room.

Finally, it was 203 he gently knocked on the door and finally, after all that waiting on the bus and having such a terrible day, he saw something worse. He looked upon his bed ridden friend and he layed there for a minute. He seemed to be in a state of iunconscnousness , that was until he sensed the presence of someone walk into the room. To his pleasant surprise it was John who walked in.

He opened his eyes,

"Mr Jenkins did I wake you?" John spoke softly, "Well how do you do young man? What are you doing here?" His voice was not the same, he sounded weak as if he were mustering up strength just to breathe as he spoke.

John grabbed the nearest chair in the room, and pulled it close to him to sit.

"Well Sir, I am here to see you. I knew something must have been wrong when I didn't see you earlier, I have been trying to get here for the last four hours."

"That's really nice of you, son. Does your mother know you are here?"

"No Sir" John replied.

If nothing else, he knew that Mr Jenkins had a sense of moral, that he envied. Something that he could never understand, especially coming from a man with such a rough childhood, and graphically tough past.

"Now you hear." As he panted for breath, "Go and call you

mother at once, and inform her of where you are, do you hear me."

Speaking seemed laborious, without a fight John pulled out his phone to call his mother. He knew that she might not have been home, since she would be working late, but he did what he was told.

After calling and informing his mom, she didn't seem overly worried, but there was something strange about that. It was as though she was just grateful to know that he was okay. She had yet to leave work, but knowing his location was nice.

CHAPTER 5: JESSE CARTER

Christina loved her sons. Both of them were her pride and joy; she missed her eldest son a great deal. Sometimes she wondered how life was for him.

As his mother was thinking about him, Jesse Carter, was at this time going through changes that would set him up to be the best navy seal officer at a very young age. He had attained the rank of chief petty officer. Although it took the average seal thirteen and a half years to accomplish that rank, he had done it in less than eight years.

Jesse wasn't the same person that left his mother's house all those years ago to join the navy. The mild mannered person that he used to be no longer existed. He formed a tough exterior that exerted from the aura that surrounded his being. He was nineteen when he left.

Eight years later; he was twenty-seven, and he still had his wide shoulder and deep voice, which complimented him as he spoke to his insubordinates. His face had fully developed a well-groomed beard to match his personality; it was jet black, just as black as the hair on his head. Like John, Jesse also had a caramel skin tone. He had gone through a metamorphosis and with each rank that he climbed, it fuelled a tenacious will to keep striving higher.

Jesse was one of the most respected men on the entire fleet, for his painstaking eye for detail and precision. He strived for excellency in everything he did. Where other men would have given up at any point he ensured that his job was not complete until he was satisfied with its quality.

He was the kind of man men dreamed of becoming. With his charismatic charm and type of personality, he outranked everyone in his class. It was a drive that was handed down to him from the streets.

Jesse wasn't always your run of the mill "good" young man. He had a past of mischievous ways that got him into problematic situations. He was always the leader type, being the "gang leader", even in primary school, he rarely if ever followed. He was a natural born leader, but rather than leading roguish males of mal-intentions, he had for the last eight years, chosen to use his natural talents and abilities to lead some of the toughest, and bravest men, in and out of many battles and there were many more to many more ahead.

Today was strange, because in over four years after having dedicated his life to his career, a picture of his mother rushed across his mind out of what seemed to be thin air, but as a hardened soldier he placed his mind back to his duties.

CHAPTER 6:
REALITY CHECK

As his mother was thinking about his brother and his brother was dismissing his own thoughts, John was next to Mr Jenkins, still talking about how he had gotten to the hospital.

He said that he was walking through a crowded street filled with people. They walked with their head held high, with no concern for the next person within their space. Children were holding their parent's hand as they went on their way merrily.

He could hear the sounds of vehicles driving through the streets, some honking their horns in impatience, exposing everyone to the smell of exhaust and pollution from all the activities of man, which only caused more damage to the environment.

As he stood there with his light blue long sleeved shirt, his soft grey dress pants and his classic brown Cambridge dress shoes and belt to match, he felt a heaviness in his chest. It was a pressure that was so intense, that it became difficult to breathe as he grabbed his chest. He was breathing deeply trying to catch his breath. Everyone walked by, without any sign of care towards what could be wrong, oblivious to his cry for help.

It was then that a man who homeless, saw what was happening and came to his rescue when he noticed Mr Jenkins slowly decline to the ground. He got up and with an outstretched arm in his tattered clothes, grabbed him, and he instructed him to cough as loud as he could.

Mr Jenkins, said that maybe if he wasn't there, he didn't know what would have happened. It was enough to keep him alive; but he still needed to get to a hospital the man just got up and went to call an ambulance as Mr Jenkins sat nearby waiting.

The humanity of mankind has dwindled through the filter of selfishness and what has come to be caught in the bodies of society is self-preservation and depravity.

No matter how much life was looked upon it was full of people with total disregard for others, but even in this bleakness, there are always shimmering glimpses of hope.

Mr Jenkins, said that once he was released from hospital, he would go looking for that man to thank him for all that he had done, it was nothing that he could pay him back for, but he sure could show his gratitude.

John was inspired by his mentor, with his wise thoughts and genuine intentions yet again. Even while he sat there listening intently, he felt the urge to check his watch for the time. It was almost 10:00 p.m. which meant he had about forty-five minutes to catch the last bus to travel back home.

Mr Jenkins saw him check his time and with an understanding motion of his hands he said, "I know it's getting late my boy and you need to be going home now."

"I am just happy you are okay." John replied with relief and genuineness. "I'll try my best to come see you tomorrow."

"You won't be able to, they are releasing me tomorrow, I only stayed over the night because the doctors said that they needed to make sure that everything was okay and that I was stabilised." Mr Jenkins responded in a very calm fatherly voice.

They said their salutations, as John started heading out the door to get home. He had been hungry all this time, and it was only getting progressively worse.

It had become apparent to him that he only ate breakfast, because he gave the cat his lunch which he could have eaten now. He didn't regret it, he had a big heart and he always felt that doing more for others made him appreciate the little things in life.

He walked out of the white tiled hospital, into the thick blackness of the night. He could see the street light which decorated the road, creating an ambience of serenity.

The nights were chilly, with biting winds that could, if unprepared, quickly eat through the warmth that one's body was mustering up in its defence.

He could feel the winds tonight and he wondered why it was so cold. The nights were generally chilly, but tonight was different; he could feel the wind as his body despreately clinged to the little warmth that remained, as the cold pressed infiltrated his body feeling as though it were passing through his bones.

Tonight was different. The generally chilly winds were even colder, he wondered why as he hunched his shoulders, put his hands in his pockets and walked faster. It was as if he could feel the winds passing through his bones.

Slowly, as he waited on transportation to arrive, he could feel his body beginning to tense, trying to reserve any warmth that his shirt and jeans could provide. He looked up at the sky and could see a bright star shining from the heavens. He could not look away; it seemed to be a shooting star, but it was brighter than any he had seen before.

He didn't believe in magic, and he certainly didn't believe in making wishes; but it was a captivating sight. Three more followed after the first in a spectacular display of blues, reds and whites across the night sky.

Little to his finite knowledge, he was experiencing a forecasted astronomical spectacle which would not occur for another millennium.

"I must say that was really cool" he muttered to himself, as he looked up wondering what in the world just happened.

Praying to finally reach home, he looked back to the almost deserted road, and could see some creeping lights approaching him. They were still faint as they were some distance away, but after a few minutes he could hear the rumbling of the engine getting closer with every second that passed.

John stood there as the bus finally reached him. It only had two other passengers, a man with an old leather brown hat, and just a plain shirt that said, *"Don't laugh cause your face is funnier than the joke."* And a woman who looked like she just came off of her work shift. She was wearing a pink waitress uniform. The driver looked out at John and shouted, "kid God must be with you because this is the last trip for the night." John scoffed, and responded with a tired, "good night."

The driver seemed to not care one bit, he looked more tired than John, and he probably was. He had blackened bags under his eyes, shaggy brown hair and very pale white skin from not being in the sun much. He had a macilent body structure, which complimented his sucked in face that looked malnourished.

The bus drove on, as both he and the other passengers resorted to their sombre moods. The journey seemed longer than usual, because he was so hungry. As each second passed, he wondered, how much closer he would be to getting home.

As he looked out into the dark night at the lights cascading over the streets as he past each light post, he noticed that the shining light created a circle of illumination, giving a small glimpse into the worlds outside of his own city.

He could see the trash cans filled with garbage and the empty street corners; but as he got closer to his own home, he could see men on the street who were wearing thick hoodies, to combat the elements. On another, there were women, who had on short skimpy clothes that revealed so much it left no room for the imagination.

The closer he got to home, the more night life he witnessed, but more importantly, the greater his desire burned within him to get out of this ruthless, uncivilized, brutish place, which was filled all kinds of characters and corrupt visionaries, and those who society rejected.

It was this place that could make a sane man go crazy.

John's stop came, and he exited with excitement to be that much closer to a warm home and a hot plate of food that he would heat up in the microwave. As he walked to his house, he noticed that there was a strange car parked outside. He had never seen this vehicle before, and he wondered who it could be, luckily it wasn't to him at all, but this wouldn't be the last time he saw that same vehicle.

The moment he stepped into his house, he headed immediately for the fridge, though the vehicle thing was strange. His mother was already home and was waiting for his arrival, so that she could go to bed. Upon entry they wished each good night and each gave a brief summary of how their day went; her with work and him with both his class experience and the hospital visit.

At this point his stomach was more important to him than anything else. He had not eaten for over twelve hours and his stomach was rumbling and crying for sustenance. He swung open the titanium doors of the refrigerator, and in it was cooked turkey which was prepared yesterday, some good seasoned rice, with some mixed veggies and a lovely salad. He couldn't complain.

He filled a plate almost bigger than himself as he popped it into the microwave to heat up. After it was heated he sat at the dinner table and devoured every bite, almost to the point of licking the plate.

He appreciated the food more than usual tonight; perhaps it was the level of his hunger that made the food taste that much better than it usually did. Rubbing his now filled belly, he got up and with a loud belch, took the plate to the kitchen as he washed it so as not to leave the sink dirty, as was his habit.

Putting the plate to dry in the dish rack, he noticed something outside the window of the kitchen; it was the same vehicle that he saw earlier, pitch black. The windows were tinted, but as he peeped out the window, he heard the sounds of a metal garbage can and the scattering sounds of plastic.

It was the sound of someone or something, rummaging through the trash can. He looked out and saw that it was a cat, which had a fluffy black coat of fur covering its body; when you looked at the face you could see yellow reflections that shone from its eyes. As it realised that it was discovered, it ran off in terrified panic.

John was a bit mad, this was the third time. Having to go and pick up the mess was a bit annoying but, he went for a fresh garbage bag as he went outside. Seeing the used tin cans and other garbage on the grass scattered around the bins, was exhausting especially after such a long day.

Before he could even complain, he heard the sound of a man's voice. It was coarse and aggressive as it resonated, causing John to wonder who it could be. The man didn't seem bothered that John had come out to pick up the garbage. It was as though he was oblivious to his presence.

While John listened he could hear the man instructing someone over the phone about their failure to complete a task, whatever that task was. After concluding the discussion over the phone, the man, walked to the vehicle with impatience in every step. John couldn't see anything but a black shadow of the man as he entered the vehicle.

The lights of the vehicle came on as they shone brightly into the darkness of the night. As he drove off, John's mind was running like a bullet train speeding down the track, trying to figure out what had just happened.

Every expression of confusion as to why all of this was happening to him today was plastered upon his face. He almost decided to leave the garbage, but he stooped down and he picked up the remains of the cat's midnight diggings.

He couldn't do anything but accept the reality of what was happening. He had class to attend in the morning and all of this was so tiring, as he finished cleaning the yard up, his movements almost looking uncoordinated and haggard, he staggered to the house, as he went to shower and brush his teeth.

As the warm water touched his caramel skin, he could only sigh heavily as he said to himself "What a day!"

It had to have been one of the worst days he had, apart from his dad dying. He stayed under the shower as the water drops flowed over his skin. Every drop seemed to make the day more bearable, and with everything that was happening, all he wanted to do was sleep.

He stepped out of the shower with his towel wrapped around him. As he looked into the sink mirror, all he could see was the image of his father, both he and his brother resembled him so much.

John grabbed his toothbrush as he took the blue, and white stripped toothpaste and placed a small bead on the bristles. It was the size of a pea as instructed by the box.

Beginning to brush, the sounds of the bristles scrubbing his teeth was the only sound that could be heard so late in the night. Scrubbing away as the fairly soft bristles rubbed over his gums, he could feel the freshness from the peppermint from the toothpaste revitalise his mouth; but It was so quiet that even a pin dropping could be heard.

As he spat the toothpaste out of his mouth, his hands reached out to turn off the tap. As he stood there, it dawned on him he forgot to ask Tim for the information to study for class tomorrow.

He thought for a minute, "it is really late and I know he will probably be asleep, so what I can do is leave extra early tomorrow and get the notes so that I can brush up on the information and do a bit more studying." At least he wouldn't have to deal with that racist old man, for another day. He had that class only on Wednesdays and Mondays, and tomorrow was Tuesday.

It was actually Tuesday already, since as it was after 12:00 a.m. The tiredness was creeping in on him as he walked over to his room to prep for the next day.

While still in his white towel, he walked over to his bag, and packed the books that he would need as well as his clothes and shoes next to each other in a neat and organised fashion. He really was a stickler for order.

When he thought he was satisfied, he took out his sleeping attire; Grey and white PJs which had the distinctive cosiness that could make even a criminal relax. As he placed his head on the pillow, his mind drifted into unconsciousness immediately. Sleep took over.

* * *

While John was sleeping, his brother was contemplating the next move in his career, which would get him the rank of a chief commander. To him, achieving was even more important that building a family, or even seeing his family. He had lost a bit of himself. Once he was a family oriented person, but things, life had changed so much in him.

Whatever the case was he needed to have a reality check and little did he know that life was about to give him a blow that he was not prepared for.

CHAPTER 7: ACCIDENT OR FATE

BEEP!, BEEP!, BEEP!, was the sound of the alarm clock as it signalled that it was time to get up. John stretched his hand out without opening his eyes, to feel for the alarm, to turn off the machine, which made sure he woke up every morning.

He still felt tired, from last night, but it was much better since he was able to at least get some rest, that was a positive. He swung his feet over the side of his bed as he shoved his feet into his bedroom slippers, as to avoid the cold floor that if unprepared, sent shivers up one's spine.

He hands came to his face to rescue his room from the smell of his morning breath, as he yawned with an exaggerated exclamation. As he got up, he realized that his mother wasn't up and that was so unlike her.

He decided to go to her room. When he entered he realised that she was still in bed and it appeared as though she was still asleep. John went to her side as he gently rubbed her back to wake her. She looked up with half opened eyes and a tired face as if to say, it's morning already!

She didn't go to sleep until I got home last night and she could use the rest after working two jobs just to make ends meet. She never had to do it when dad was home, but after his death, she had become both mother and father.

Little by little, John came to a fuller appreciation for everything his mom did, and all the sacrifices that she made, just to put food on the table. He may have lived in the slums of the city, but he was aristocratic at heart. Everything that he did, the way that he did it, was to bring his thoughts of himself into reality, and this really was coming into fruition every day that passed.

Even his response at school yesterday, was born out of such a magnificent respect for himself, and his own ideals that to argue with a self-righteous, egotistical racist with no understanding of the humanity to him was inconsequential.

His ideology was one that was based upon, the true understanding of what mankind ought to be, and with this came opposition of those who could not find the grounds to break into the metamorphosis of mind and conscious living. This was the inhibition of the human psyche, and the more he personified his thoughts, the more he became transcendental in thought.

John, didn't place much of his thoughts on his professor, whose mentality was stunted by its own discretion towards evolution; but rather, he emphasised his actions, and internal monologue within the confines of the knowledge that was to come from his psychology class that he took to better understand the human disposition.

He got ready as he usually did and in doing so, he went to shower and put his clothing on. In today's style list, he evaluated the colour scheme of his clothing choices and decided upon something more plain.

John took the light grey jacket that was hanging on the rack for a while, on the front it bore the logo of his university, with an emblem to match. His jacket hid the grey and white shirt which hid the black bold letters arranged to say, "Water the mind, and grow seeds of thoughts." It was one a pretty cool shirt if you asked anyone, and John personally liked it. As for pants selection he chose the soft khaki pants. He grabbed his sneakers which were black and grey to compliment what he was wearing.

With his clothes finally on and bag on his back, he headed out, but not without checking on his mother, once again he asked, "Mom are you okay?"

She hadn't been like this before so it was a bit alarming. He went to her bedside and shook her awake. As she came out of the daze that usually comes after being awaken from a deep sleep, he asked her once more, "Are you okay?"

Her response was nothing shy of concerning, "I don't know, but I'll be fine, just a bit tired." "Mother, are you sure that you are okay?" John replied with concern in his voice, as he watched his mother and every line that creased her face.

He could see that her age was truly catching up with her, as she gracefully aged over time. He loved her dearly though he did not spend enough time with her. Childhood proved to him that his mother loved him.

His mom, looked at the clock as she realized the time of the day and, that spurred her to hustle to get up as she emphasised that he should go to class. John wasn't fully convinced but he accepted it and, went on his way, not feeling fully sure about what was happening.

As he walked to the bus terminal, he noticed a twenty-dollar bill on the ground. As no one was there he picked up the money and with one swift move, he looked around to see if anyone would claim it, as a few other people came and looked for the terminal to also catch the bus to get to their designated workplaces and educational institutions.

After a few minutes when no one came to claim or even inquire about the money, he pocketed it and went over to the seats that were provided to sit; but upon looking at its nasty brown colour with black stains that resembled that of faeces he objected to the idea, his face filled with disgust and disdain for the condition of this public seating.

As he stood there, he could hear the sounds of the tires rolling on the tar of the street, as the wind followed along with the engine spewing out its call.

There was the smell of exhaust as an older vehicle, drove

past with a cloud of white smoke coming from its tailpipe. The thick blanket of combustion coated the air with hazardous and obnoxious fumes. John gave a small cough, as the smell hit the back of his throat. It was almost immediate when he grabbed for the collar of his jacket to pull over his nose, to try to restrict the smell from getting into his nasal passage.

As the vehicle reached a distance away, the fumes dissipated into thin air, following the vehicle like a hoard of bees to a provocateur of the hive; and as the fumes left, so was the need for the jacket to cover the bottom half of his face.

Finally, it was time for the bus to come. He impatiently awaited its arrival. The sound of the brakes coming to a halt, expressed with a hiss, as the doors swung open with whoosh and metal hit against hardened plastic.

John stepped into the bus hoping that he would see a familiar face, but instead, it was the man from yesterday, who originally gave him the negative news about Mr Jenkins.

He looked at him once again and noticed the fuzz growing on his face. Without warning, he looked at John, and asked "So how is he?"

John was almost, shocked to hear him ask that question, but he figured maybe the driver knew something which he did not. The doors of the bus swung closed, behind John, as it pulled off from the curb and onto the road to travel to its destinations.

"How did you know I went to see him?" John asked, especially after the weird events of last night, he felt on edge, although he could not explain why.

"I saw you yesterday; do you remember the accident that happened on the road?" The man questioned, "Well, yes I heard about it."

"Are you sure you just heard about it?" John was starting to get suspicious of the questions, and asked "Were you following me?"

"No not at all, I just know that you were there, because I too was at the hospital. "The boy that was rushed to the hospital was my son."

"What do you mean was?" John replied.

"Well, my son was a part of that accident, and last night, I saw you leave there, I couldn't go and see Jenkins, because I was more concerned about my son. Well he passed away this morning"

John couldn't help but sympathize with him. He had what people would say was a genuine heart. He knew there wasn't much he could do, or say, but he gave his heartfelt sympathies.

The man didn't show any more or any less of an expression on his face from before, it was almost vacant of any ability to express emotion, which was strange, especially someone going through something like this; but he tried to rationalize it, and came to the conclusion that he could just be suppressing or abating his emotional response.

With his eyes fixed on the road, the driver ended the conversation by saying I hope the old guy is alright. In John's eyes he wasn't that young to begin with, but he could hear in the guy's voice a minor playfulness as he said that; which caused John to chuckle a bit inside.

John realised that this man was just trying to cope with his emotional distress, but was unwilling to deal with it head on; and he understood this process too well. There are days when it would be better to ignore the fact as though it never happened, than to deal with it.

He knew that feeling all too well.

It didn't matter; he just walked to his seat, though he felt a prick in his heart toward this man's situation. As he reached to the front of his school, he exited the bus and went about his business.

He knew it was a new day and anything that happened yesterday was nothing more than a once forgotten tomorrow. And today, he would bear the stresses of this day, for the weight of yesterday must be left in the past. He had a journey to continue towards his future.

Any and all baggage which would not give way to achievement of his goal, were left without a second thought.

Stepping onto the campus grounds, he walked quickly with his head held high, pep in his step and confidence that was so strong you could smell it emanating from his musk.

His favourite lecturer was quite a remarkable woman, she was one of the top psychologists around, and her name was Ramona Brown. She was in her mid-thirties, and she had accomplished much in her short life so far; with many awards behind her name, which gave her a level of prestige.

She had a beautiful glossy sheen to her long black flowing hair, which was always well done. She had an hour glass figure, which she maintained through her rigorous exercise regime, that she took very seriously.

John always thought of her as a gorgeous woman, but his admiration was more about her achievements and her intelligence than her physical features. John was so driven to achieve, that he never had a relationship with anyone, and everyone that came, he found some way to distance himself. Somehow, with Ms Brown, it was different.

The crazy thing was that even though he didn't realize it, she found him to be attractive. She understood that he was an intelligent young man with a high level of potential and she admired that.

As much as possible he tried his best to ignore his feelings towards Ms Brown. This would be the beginning of a long story; one that he was not ready to sign up for.

When class had officially begun and he sat in his usual seat, he prepared himself to absorb all the information that was about to delivered. He would devour every little fragment of information.

Sometimes in class, she would ask questions, and in a brief moment, there would be some eye contact between the two of them, but it was never more than just a few seconds. John did not pay too much attention to it.

Quite often when she would call on him to answer those questions as if she already knew he would be able to respond accurately, and she simply wanted to verify that her assumptions were right.

At every chance that he was given to expound upon his consistent work ethic and immense intelligence he did so with a confidence that exuberated from his answers, and she found this intriguing.

Class continued as usual, and she gave out a new assignment to keep them busy. They all listened, some more involved than others, she spoke to all, but with John she expected more.

At the end of class when she had finally ended the lecture for the day, John left, to go to his other class, as he went from class to class, his mind would go back to the bus driver's situation; even more than that, he realized today was one day that he found himself thinking about Ms Brown more than usual.

Every class that he went to seemed to be better than the last, and as the day drew closer to an end, he couldn't wait to get home for once. It was almost as though there was a lingering contentment in the air that was traceably linked to how he was feeling.

This morning, he made up his mind that he would have a good day from the moment he stepped off the bus and since then, it seemed that his decision materialised into existence.

His final class was truly great; he could almost feel the information being absorbed as he ended the day. Strangely enough he had not seen his best friend for the entire day and that wasn't like him at all. Tim wasn't the delinquent type to skip classes, sure he wasn't always punctual, but missing class was not something that he was prone too.

He took the moment to go outside as the lecture was going on, and he pulled out his phone. He could see the background picture of a black and white panda bear on his screen, just as he swiped up to open it. As he entered his password, he opened the call log and called Tim.

Tim answered the phone with a tired tone.

"Hello".

"Tim, are you okay" John questioned,

"Yeah, I am fine"

"Why aren't you at class, I haven't seen you all day man."

"Man, I am in the nurse's office, I saw you this morning."

"Bro, why are you there" John asked beginning to get concerned.

"I think I got a stomach bug, and I just came here to check myself out before, I really might be sick."

John replied "Okay", as he started his walk towards the nurse's office to see if his best friend was okay. As it turned out, Tim wasn't looking too good, but there wasn't much else he could do at that point than to just look at him.

"Man you look awful, what's wrong with you?"

"Didn't I just speak with you over the phone?" the rhetorical sarcasm rang through Tim's voice weakly.

They both chuckled at their initial response after seeing each other for the first time for the day.

There was no doubt about Tim's condition; though he had enough energy to be a wisecrack as usual, John could see that he really wasn't in the best of health.

John decided that he would wait on him, and make sure he got home safely. Unlike John though Tim, never knew his father; he was raised by a proud single woman with wide hips and a personality to match. She expressed the importance of education from a very young age and this was personified within Tim's being.

While they walked out of the building and headed off the campus, you could feel the cooling winds that came about because of the cascading clouds above. Growing in size and darkening in colour, the presence of the inevitable showers of rain signalled to all those that were under its umbrella that they were about to be doused with water.

Before they could get a moment to think about the impending shower, the faint sound of rain began in the distance, and the smell of freshly fallen rain perfumed the air. The sounds of rain came closer and the two ran for shelter to keep from getting wet.

The rain didn't just fall when it finally reached them, it poured. It poured so much that it started to flood, and the men had to decide whether to stay and be trapped by the weather or try to get home.

They looked at each other and with one unanimous head nod. They ran in the rain, trying to use their bags to protect them as they ran from shelter to shelter.

In John's bag was his laptop which he almost forgot was in there as the pouring rain started penetrating the thick exterior of his bag. Fortunately for him, his bag was given to him by his brother years ago, and it had some waterproofness that prevented it from being soaked all the way through. This safeguarded his laptop and they continued their endeavours to reach home.

As they got closer to the bus stop they were both wet and dripping with water. This made the bus driver hesitant to transport them, but since he understood the situation, he gave them a pass.

Upon their journey home, a sudden approaching vehicle which had lost control due to the wet and slippery road was hurtling towards the bus that Tim and John were in. It was a yellow Jeep with black trim, coming with chaotic speed. The passengers all started screaming as everyone noticed that the vehicle was coming too quickly to divert from hitting the bus.

Miraculously, just as the bus was about to be hit with immense force that would have probably have knocked it off the road, the Jeep made an abrupt turn that saved both vehicles from colliding in what surely would have been a deadly accident.

Everyone was traumatized, as those who knew each other tried to comfort one another. It really was a moment to be scared, but John and Tim could do nothing but sit there in shock as they just witnessed their own "movie".

This was a term they used when something was too surreal to be true. After about ten minutes, it finally came to John's realisation that he once again almost witnessed his own death, and this caused him to start thinking about it deeply.

This wasn't his first taste at an eminent threat to his life. When he was about nine years old, he could remember falling into the deep end of the pool, while yet not being a strong swimmer. As he thought about it, a feeling of melancholy, washed over him like a wave engulfing his entire being. "Why were all of these things happening to him?" he wondered. At every turn there seemed to be a different problem. It was as if the universe played the symphony of perpetuating sorrows lately, and it seemed daunting to even try to figure why.

John clenched his fist as he looked up, he had not realised he was doing it, but more and more, he hardened his determination to do what he set his mind to doing and it could be seen on his face, but unlike his usual, serious demeanour this was a calm relaxed expression.

While John was there going through his existential crisis, his brother, was facing a threat from terrorist forces on the other side of the world.

Things seemed bleak as Jesse, in his full attire attended a meeting with other military heads to discuss the potential threat that was coming their way.

On one side, John was going through his roughest week in a long time, but on the other side, his brother was preparing for potential terrorist attacks that could bring about the loss of innocent lives.

As Jesse, walked around with his uniform decorated with many pins, representing his achievements and valour; he pointed to the screen which had a strategic plan to infiltrate the enemy camp and attack it from the inside out.

Jesse needed everyone to be in agreement so the plan could be implemented. There were the sounds of generals murmuring amongst themselves, wondering if, they should move forward with the plan, or whether they should dismiss it and go to another.

After a moment, a man dressed in a neatly cut black suit, a white shirt and a black silk tie walked into the room, and as he walked in, a hush fell over the room. The room was dimly lit to accommodate the projections on the screen. The air thickened, they could not see his face until the light was returned.

As Jesse and the other men wondered who this man was; John was wondering what to do next.

CHAPTER 8: MOM

The bus continued to carry all its passengers to their respective destinations. When John got to his, he went home, as he normally would, before venturing out to where ever he saw fit while his mother worked; today there was something strange, as he took out his keys to open the door he realised that it was already opened, which was strange as the door is always locked, because the neighbourhood was known for its thieves.

John opened the door all the way with caution, as he looked into the house. As he looked around the house, it seemed fine, until he heard the sound of a pot in the kitchen. His heart rate quickly increased as he wondered who it could be.   He crept silently towards the origin of the sound, and as he did so, he slowly peered into the kitchen and to his surprise, it was his mother.

"Mom what are you doing home? It's only three in the afternoon." John questioned his mother who looked unusually tired. It was the first time in weeks, since he really took notice of his mom's appearance, and it wasn't until he looked closely he could see that she was looking unusually tired, but not the kind of tired that presented its look upon someone who just finished a sixteen-hour shift. This tired was the kind that looked similar to when someone is ill, the pale white look in her eyes, and the fatigue that distorted her face was to the point of almost being sucked in. It was alarming, as John looked at his mother; she barely had the strength to move.

"What's wrong?" John spoke with tenderness towards his mother. "I'm alright baby, just a little tired." She replied.

In fact, John's mother had been sick for months, but because they had rarely seen each other, for more than a few minutes at a time, because of the long days of work, he had not realised that she was not recovering as she should. John knew as he looked at his mother that whatever it was, everything was at its worst.

He stretched his hands forward as he embraced his mother with the most loving hug he could muster. He could feel his heart breaking seeing his mother like this. She hugged him back with a faint grasp as she rubbed his back trying to make him feel like everything was alright.

As they stood there for a moment, tears came to her eyes as she looked up at her son, whom she watched grow up, with a face that mirrored his father. She held him a little tighter with the little strength that she could muster up. As her ears rested against her son, she could hear the soft sounds of his heart beating rhythmically. She inhaled deeply as she lifted herself with her hands while still holding his sides. She looked up at him. "I love you my son, she whispered and no matter what, you'll always be my son."

As she leaned forward she could feel her legs giving way to the weight of her body and the feeling of weakness. Her eyelids slowly descended, as she began to lose consciousness. It pounced upon her like a predator to its prey just before its final execution.

Falling forward into her son's hands, she fainted as John stretched his hands out to grab his mother before she could hit the floor.

She had completely lost cognizance. John placed her limp body gently on the floor, his mind raced through a thousand thoughts simultaneously as he hurried for the phone and dialled 911 to get the emergency department.

There was a slight panic in his voice, which caused his once deep voice to rise in pitch that matched his level of worry. It was as if fear started to take control of his once stoic demeanour, but this was actually happening. He urged the man on the line, to please send help, "Hurry!! Please!!" as he cried out before hanging up the phone.

He waited for what felt like forever for the ambulance finally arrived, by this time, he had gotten a damp rag to wipe her face and placed a pillow under her head to elevate her.

She remained unconscious, the entire time, but to John's surprise, as the ambulance arrived, his mother began to return to her awakened state. You could see within his eyes a moment of peace as he saw his mother open her eyes.

"Mom" he exclaimed as the EMTs reached, "they're here, you're going to be just fine, don't worry about a thing okay!" he said as he went to let them in.

The men came into the room with a stretcher and they wasted no time in getting her inside the ambulance, which had its red and white lights spinning. As John got in the back, he felt the tug of the vehicles G-force pushing him towards the closed back door.

He swung his hands out to hold onto anything sturdy that might be able to help him keep his balance, as the vehicle danced through traffic, with its loud siren blaring. They were heading to the same hospital that Mr Jenkins was at, he would go see him, after he knew for sure that his mom was alright.

It seemed like a rather unfortunate few days as one event was followed by another, as if someone outside of his reach was conjuring up all these chaotic events, but for what purpose, was it for the entertainment of some being from another universe, time, and space?

His mind was in complete disarray as they drove down the highway, speeding towards the hospital. While the vehicle continued she lost consciousness once more, and would black out for the rest of the night until the doctors aided her in regaining her consciousness once again.

The ride seemed unbearable. It was worse than the hours

he had to spend just trying to see Mr Jenkins. The only thing is with this one he didn't know what was happening and every second felt like an hour, as all he could do was pray, "I hope she'll be okay." He said with belief that maybe, he might be heard by the being whom he thought might be putting him through this ordeal, as some form of entertainment.

He sighed heavily.

The ambulance drove onto the hospital grounds, and as they reached the emergency doors, they pulled his mother out with a hurried caution, as nurses came rushing to the aid of this woman to begin figuring out the cause of her illness.   Her frail lifeless body being carried to the room to be examined laid lifelessly with a shallow raising and falling of her chest, which pointed to life still being present.

John had not yet figured out what he was truly feeling, and it could be seen upon his blank emotionless daze of an expression. His mother was rushed away; he went to the waiting area.

While he was sitting, his mind raced as he tried to determine what exactly it is that he should be doing, his thought rapidly coming and going to a syncopated rhythm. While he was sitting there he could see the multitude of sick people, who were in need of attendance, as well as the busy medical staff in their white scrubs walking around organising the hospital and its patients.

For a brief moment, as he looked his mind went silent as if in expectation of some grand thought to help with the situation; and it was then, almost audibly, the idea of calling his brother came to mind.

Stopping for a moment, before even grabbing his phone, he realised that he truly had not spoken to his brother in four years. As any rational person would, he began to assess the situation and the decision he was about to make.

He began by asking himself "what if he doesn't have the same number? What if he didn't call or write because, he didn't want to speak with us?"

As quickly as the thoughts came he would reply internally, "we are his family and it doesn't matter if he does or does not want to speak with us, I need him to come."

John pulled his phone out of his pocket with a suddenness that reflected his calm excitement.

As he looked through his phone for the number that was there before, he could hear the dial tone as he clicked on the number attached to his brother's name.

The phone began to ring, as his heart began beating increasingly faster in anticipation. His eyes darted around the room as the phone, continued to ring without an answer. It continued to ring, but without avail, it reached the operator; just as he hung the phone up his determination kicked in and he hit the redial button.

He summoned all his faculties to attention as he tried to remedy a solution to both his mother's ailment, and his brother's family neglect. The phone reached its fourth ring, as a deep voiced man answered the phone. It was definitely his brother, John stood there shocked that he still had this number.

John quickly explained what was happening to mother, and how he needed his assistance. His brother was silent throughout the entire conversation as John spoke. There were no murmurs to signify that he was listening, but as John wrapped up all that he had to say, the only response that came before Jesse hung up the phone was "See you in the morning" then he heard a click.

John looked at his phone almost in disbelief with what just happened. Jesse never even acknowledged anything he said and it almost disappointed him, for as quickly as the feeling came, it drifted away, as he consoled himself with the thought that, he may actually be coming.

A bit of excitement came over him, but also a feeling of disenchantment. His choice was not to be disheartened and he came back to his senses, because at this time he needed to be in full readiness for his mom. As he stood there he saw someone that he truly wanted to talk to with, it was Mr Jenkins. He had plans to see him later but instead it seemed that he came to see John.

He had just been released and was in good spirits to see his morning passenger, who was like a son to him.

"Hey, Mr Jenkins" John said as he walked to him with half smile on his face. He was feeling a bit defeated, as he walked over to him. There were two comfortable chairs, where they were standing, available to anyone who wished. John beaconed for them to sit, which Mr Jenkins gladly accepted.

As they sat there, John went through every detail that he wanted to tell him from before, going as far back as the class with that racist man and everything before, he also told him about the present situation with his mother and his brother who would be coming.

"Hmmm." Mr, Jenkins replied
Before unleashing his wise words to John which seemed to calm his spirits and give him a sense of a peace in his mind.

Just then a nurse walked up to John as she apologised for disturbing the conversation. "Are you John Carter?" She asked.

John relied with an affirmative answer. She began to explain to him that his mother had developed a very rare form of a disease that has been making her sick, for months. She explained that persons who developed this disease would rarely survive the ordeal.

His heart began to melt with disbelief as the words vibrated through the air to the outside of his ear, his auricle. As the sound-waves danced upon his auditory receptors, he knew that he was powerless to the present situation, and by this he listened with estranged intensity.

As the nurse concluded her diagnosis, he stretched forward his hand slowly to indicate that he had heard enough, and that he needed a moment to digest everything that she had said.

He made an about turn as he walked with his head high, almost as if to suggest to the world that everything would be okay, even though inside it felt as though a tumultuous storm had arisen over the pacific seas with furious anger; in his utter help-lessness, he gatherer the strength to force his will, to subject it to his own means of behaviour. If he could not conjure up the necessary resources to enable his world to be fixed, he could at least, conjure the strength to change his reaction.

John, took a deep breath as he walked away to find a seat to think about everything that he just heard. With his mind being soothed by his will to not panic, to not succumb to the reality, he gained a new strength. Strength from reserves that he never would have known existed, until this very moment,

For a moment he closed his eyes his moment, and when he opened it, it was nine pm. What seemed like seconds became hour, when he opened his eyes, with his heart beating quickly; he walked to the nurse from his slumber and requested to see his mother.

They would have to hold her for a few days before they could release her. John said nothing about the ordeal, but that insisted to see her.

The nurse beckoned him to follow her as she carried him to his destination. He opened the door, and to his amazement, she was awake, fully alert.

She reached out her hands for her son, who will love in his eyes and concern, walked over and hugged her gently, as if to say that everything would be alright.

As they embraced one another, John whispered, "Why didn't you tell me, about your illness?

"I didn't want you to worry my child. This is of my concern, and there isn't anything we can do but do the necessary practices and hold things get better."

As the words came out of her mouth, he could see tears welling up in her eyes. As the air went silent between them and the moment quiet, a tear came to her eye and she looked at her son with an apology that no words could express sufficiently.

She looked away, almost as if ashamed, not ashamed at not telling him, but ashamed that she was sick and that he had to see her like this. She had always been a source of strength. When hard times came, she was ready to smother it with even harder work, when troubles raged; she burned with the frenzy of determination.

It is no wonder; her son spurred the attitude of persistence, of sheer will and willpower. She was no better than his father, a man of will and honour, a man who would have pulled the moon closer to earth, if it meant doing what was best for his family; but now, it was just mother, and she fell saddened to know that she could not be what she thought what was necessary.

As the moment lingered they said their good night and I love you and John made his way to go home.

As soon as John reached home, he could hardly stand. His mind was exhausted from wrestling with his thoughts, and his energy levels were depleted to almost nothingness.

Although he was tired, he grabbed his towel, went to the bathroom, showered, went to eat, brushed his teeth and set his alarm to browse through his work and potential work, that would come up in that this man's class tomorrow.

He set his alarm for 3am, so that he could have a full step on the day, as this would give him the advantage of reinforcing what he knew and invigorating new thought and theories. With his time set and his objective solidified within his mind he went to sleep, but not before blurring through all that had happened that day.

Not long after he was asleep, and just as he had planned woke to implement his strategy at being the best in school. No amount of troubles would stop his drive to achieve, to do better than his fellow colleagues.

At exactly, 5:25 am he went back to bed to get some rest before class; but as he went to sleep, he found himself being awakened to not his alarm at 7am, but rather the sounds of heavy rapping on the front door.

John jumped up from his sleep, because only the police rapped like this and he could not understand why they would be there. John looked briefly at the clock to check the time, and he noticed it was only 6:30 am.

As he walked downstairs, unhappily at his guest, when he looked out the door to see who it was, he was shocked to see who it was.......

John opened the door, and the silences between the two were so thick that one could almost cut it with a butter knife.

"It's been a while John; I see you've grown up. You look just like your father."

"He was your father too, Jesse" John replied as he watched his brother in his fully decked out uniform.

Jesse, didn't waste any time in formalities, he spoke with direct specifics. He asked for mother's whereabouts, her condition and what could be done.

There was not a moment to think anything other than what was being presented. John could see that Jesse had changed in more ways than one, and it almost scared John that this was not the brother he remembered, the brother whom he grew with, went to the movies with, and ate cotton candy with.

For a moment, inside he cried for his brother's humanness, for it seemed to vanish, but as soon as John answered all his inquiries, a black vehicle had mysteriously appeared in front of the house.

It was the exact same vehicle from the night when John was taking out the garbage. The windows were so tinted that he couldn't make out anyone or anything that was behind those blackened windows.

John's face of confusion, was expressed to the point that it was impossible to not acknowledge it, so when Jesse looked as him, he walked up to him and rested his hand on his shoulder.

"Things aren't the same anymore." Jesse said as he looked John in the eyes.

With little awareness to what was happening, Jesse explained everything. He had been fighting an unknown war, as they infiltrated the enemy's database; but shortly they had been detected and were once again blocked from the server.

They were concerned that they might have been tracked from the wormholes through which they had to go through. It was their hope that they would have not been, but for safe keeping, vehicles were sent to watch the families of all who were involved in this digital warfare.

The night John saw his supposed protectors for the first time, was the night that they received confirmation that they did not have to continue their watch, as news had spread about the success from the mission to collect the information.

They had retrieved enough information through their small access to the servers, that it showed enough strategies and hidden reports to protect them from any attacks, and because of this, the fear of the potential disaster had been averted.

John understood everything that was happening, and he accepted what was being said. And deep within his heart, he knew that there was more that was not being said, but more than anything else, he cared more for his mother at this point and nothing mattered more.

Jesse now being home brought John both solace and sadness, and as his emotion were intermingled, he clenched his teeth.

He had to attend to his mother and in no way would that be stopped, and while Jesse went to see their mother; he went to school to deal with that man once more.

With his head held high and his emotions at bay he resurrected his tenacity to do his best in everything that he could to be where he needed to be.

He met up with Tim as soon as he got to school, he looked and felt much better than yesterday, and that brought a sense of reassurance to his heart.

He went to his first class for the day, as this repugnant man, said good morning to every other student but John, and it didn't bother him one bit, as his nonchalant attitude did not even recognise the insult of the professor.

He did notice that this man, who was looking for a particular response, after not even receiving recognition for his attempt to disrespect John earlier was a bit annoyed, as the expression on his face expressed distaste and a hint of disappointment.

A smile creased his face as he walked to his seat, and with his back turned to the professor he could feel his piercing gaze locked onto him.

Nothing in the world was going to stop him from accomplishing what was needed, and now with his mother sick he had a new found desire that made his previous fervour seemed tame.

It was with this new desire, that seemed to make everything that was explained during this class and all his other classes that much more interesting. It was as though challenges gave him the will to learn.

What was strange was that professor Stevens did not pick on him today, he didn't even acknowledge his presence, and that did not bother John one bit. Today seemed to be a really good day, as he soaked in every ounce of information like water to a sponge. His mind racing over the information, perusing the board for all that he could learn.

He noticed that there was a new option to the problem that was written on the board and with the feeling of inspiration, he began to write, write as if there was some new formula that could change the fabrics of human society.

It was one of the rare moments that spurred from random inspiration; the kind of inspiration that could be associated with many of the inventions that populated the now modern.

It was breath-taking, as his hands danced along the pages of the book in which he wrote the about the changes in the human psyche that could release new potential reaches into the untapped areas of human development.

Professor Stevens was oblivious to the discovery that was captured with this young man, in his class. The unleashed brainpower that was already laced with determination and brilliance, if fostered would enable many to better their quest for achieving advancement.

For a moment, as he was lost in his new found excitement of thought and discovery failed to realize that the class had come to its completion.

While he sat there engrossed within his work and the movement of his finger moving at a steadily unending pace, the sounds of hardened shoe soles came tapping closer as the sounds of footsteps, gained proximity.

He did not notice the professor drawing near to him as he continued oblivious to his surroundings. It was strange, that not even Tim came to tell him of what was happening; but Tim knew better than to disturb John whenever he had a mentally stimulating idea.

Tim, had seen John in this exact state before, when they were younger, and because he had caused John to lose his focus as he was in the thick of it, the reaction that he gave, engrained itself within his mind to never repeat that action again, and so he left him to do what he needed to do until whenever he would be out of his spell like trance.

The professor walked up to John as he wrote unknowingly. He leaned over and looked upon the work that he had been writing, and to his amazement, he saw theories that could potentially be a revolutionary; but as he continued to observe his writing and following the formulas and theories, John looked up and with a swift flick of his wrist, he shut the book, grabbed his bag and all his other possessions as he headed for the door.

"Mr Carter" the professor blurted out as John tried to quickly remove himself from his presence.

As John paused to see what he wanted, Mr Stevens looked at the boy with a curiosity. Who would have taught, this black young man could conjure up such complex theories and develop such a field of thought?

"What were you writing sir? What evoked those ideas?" He asked John.

He remained silent for a moment, as his mind ran through the far expanse of potential trouble that could result from answering this question; but this time, the professor genuinely questioned him, not as a means to slander him, but to come to an understanding of this young black boy's mind.

For the first time, his dislike for the skin tone of this John was not a factor in his communication. While the sounds of silence ringed loudly, through their nonverbal communication in the empty auditorium of chairs and desks that inhabited the room; the thought dawned upon John that his mother was still in the hospital and he had not looked or even checked on her today.

He placed everything aside as he politely excused himself from the conversation. This was further carried through as he turned around and walked out the door to go check his mother.

CHAPTER 9: ILLNESS

When John walked off of the campus he, didn't know that he was starting his first rounds of normalizing his life around the illness.

For the first two weeks, his brother stayed and looked over his mother, despite the fact of the illness that now fixed itself upon her.

She seemed to have plateaued in her state, and it wasn't showing signs of betterment.

Every day John would go visit his mother, hoping that, that day would be the day that he would be told that she was doing better and that things would begin to look up. But no matter how much he hoped it seemed to be getting worse, rather than better.

There were times that the natural progression of frustration encased him like a whirlwind engulfing a home from its rooted foundation.

The agonizing struggle of lack of funding and school fees had brought a new meaning to the word determination.

John decided to get a part-time Job to assist with the bills. He felt the need to do his part despite the fact that his brother was sending money to help out after he left.

He would send monies to assist with the bills for medical expenses, as well as the monies for basic standard living, and every time that John earned his wages he would set it aside to further his future.

He would take the money and place it in a pink coated piggy bank that his dad gave to him when he was only seven years old.

He did consistently as it would be essential in his quest to be a better man, and to begin building the foundation of a better life for his mother now and his family to come.

Months now he had been sticking to this routine, from school to his Job. His brother still sent money to them. It seemed like he was doing it as a means to make up for not visiting.

The black vehicle would show up from time to time, as it probably did before, but he actually took notice of when they arrived for the first couple of weeks, before he paying attention altogether.

Jesse called the house religiously every day to request information on the status of their mother. And just like John, he too was powerless in the situation, even with all the ranks that he had achieved.

Imagining the realities of the fickle and frivolous nature of the pursuits of life started to weigh on Jesse's psyche. He didn't want to lose his mother to this, not at the time when he was winning the war and, was soon about to receive another promotion.

Jesse had called the phone of his past home, for the routine check-up since mom went into the hospital, but today it was different.
When John finally answered the ringing phone, he heard the voice of Jesse, there was an uncanny tone of morbidity that could never be mistaken.

I know mom is not doing well, I just called the hospital and the news isn't good.

"Have you heard anything?" He asked. "I can't say that I have, what's wrong?" John inquired as his heart rate increased with such a pulsating feeling in the muscle in his chest he could hear the sound of his own heart beating.

"They said that mom is going to need to stay in the hospital for a bit longer." John tensed as he listened to his brother's voice both with reassurance and also concern for her.

Everything seemed to be going in the opposite direction.

When John placed the phone back on the hook, he went to look for a seat. The nearest one was in the living room. As he sat his mind began drifting through a tunnel of thoughts, down the river of dreams. Sitting there, under the weight of his emotions he drifted off to sleep.

It was the dream that he had been having over and over again, and this time it seemed like it was even more real than before.

He woke up in a cold sweat as exasperated breaths resonated from his mouth. The dream always ended with him, staring down the metal frame of the front of the truck, before it came rushing to him.

He felt haunted by this dream, with its reoccurring imagery. He was yet to understand the dream, but it would be revealed to him in time.

Days went by, with him taking in the magnitude of the illness, as he went to and from school, his part-time job and the hospital to check in on his mother as if it was a new found ritual.

He had not been himself lately, the moments of time seemed to have slipped as he intermingled with exhaustion and determination.

At every turn, no matter the negative thoughts, he found himself remembering why he was doing this in the first place.

It was a Wednesday, when John had gone to the hospital, and seeing his mother lying on the bed motionless as she slept peacefully, that almost sent him into rage. He could not understand, why if there was a God in heaven, why he was doing this, why all his efforts to be better than his fellow peers and surrounding neighbours, were faced with adversity and sadness on every side.

In that moment it was as if he could feel a gentle breeze, pass through the hospital.

It was strange, because not only was there a breeze in a closed building, but what was even more strange was that as the wind blew, he heard a voice, distinct from anyone else's, in the room that was occupied by only himself and his mother and she was fast asleep.

He looked around the room, and even stepped out into the vacant hallway, just to make sure that he wasn't losing his mind, or that there truly was not someone, somewhere else maybe whispering.

There was no other person around, no busy hallways, no other sound but his own thoughts and the sound of his mother's soft breathing.

He pulled the chair next to his mother, but this time he was sure that the voice that he heard was truly heard. It said "The water is not a drop unless compared to an ocean; a gush isn't a breeze unless it is compared to a tornado. What are you?

He paused, almost frozen in the seat next to his mother. He had not moved, neither had she, the only movement that showed life, was the rising and falling of her chest.

When he finally recovered from the shock at what just happened. He packed up and went home. From the hospital to the house, he sensed that something was going to happen, he couldn't tell whether it was good or bad, but what he was sure about, was the fact that despite his reluctance, he wanted to understand what that dream meant.

Even more than the dream, where did the voice come from and what did it mean?

CHAPTER 10: HOME FOR CHRISTMAS

Weeks had passed since his mother's illness and hospitalisation. He was still working part-time and Jesse was still sending money. John was still discovering new formulas to understanding the theory he stumbled upon, as well as the trying to understand the new strange occurrences that had been arising lately.

It had been about two months, since the illness, and today there was hope of her getting better. The doctors had been saying that she was gaining momentum in building a resistance to the illness, and it buoyed his spirits as he heard this fantastic news.

For the first time in weeks, John had walked with the pep in his step that he once had, and it was noticeable. Every day since the ordeal, Tim was right there by his side as he came to school.

When John saw Tim, he quickened his pace to let him know that things are finally getting better. Although, it had not yet been better, he felt a shift in the atmosphere of things and it gave him a hope he could not explain.

Tim quickly pulled him to the side as he approached him, and he asked him…"is everything Okay? You seem…. different, and I don't know what to make of it."

John replied with an affirmative, "I think everything is alright." Tim smiled with a genuine happiness for his best friend. He had not seen him happy in two months, and he was elated to see him now, more gleeful.

With so much time gone, it was now time for exams. He couldn't believe it, and he had really been pushing many nights and days just to be able to keep his grades up, work, and look after his mother, and now it all seemed to be worth it.

Over the past two weeks, they prepped for exams, with everything within them, Tim came over, even more than before as they studied tirelessly, even when he visited his mother at the hospital he would take along some schoolwork and study in the room with his mother.

John knew, everything was going to be alright.

Jesse still called as he normally would, now his mission which was so volatile so many months ago, had turned in their favour, as the heat of war seemed to have died down to the victory of their foe's defeat.

John and Jesse spoke for hours, and it was the one time since his return that he felt like his brother was now back to being the person who he knew before. This was what he missed, what he longed for.

It was this person, whom he so wanted to be growing up, and knowing he was still there gave him some reminiscence on old times before the chaos that was life. Neither of them knew life would take all the unexpected turns that were possible in their present reality. Who knew if they would bounce through it?

It was wonderful knowing that there was now such freshness to the air, as the toxicity of dread which seemed to have arisen within recent times, began to float away effortlessly as the conductor to the events of the human race moved the universe to the command of His hands.

❋ ❋ ❋

It wasn't long before mother was out of the hospital. It was December, and the traditions of Christmas were in the air, as the festivals and meal compelled the spirit of giving.

For the first time in a long awaited time, John sat at the table with his mother and brother. There had been so much to catch up on, that was not able to be addressed over the phone.

Jesse looked over at John intensely, without a blink or shift of emotion. Before a word was uttered out of his mouth, he could see something in Jesse that was different from when he first came.

As he stared, Jesse looked over at his mother who was doing so much better, and the sensation of happiness came upon him. It was as if he could not hold back the emotions as he said, "I love you both, and it is nice to be home."

It was random, but it was welcomed as mother for the first time since dad died, expressed tears.

My mom stretched out her hand as she touched her eldest's hand, softly replying, "We love you too, it's nice to have you home again."

As the emotions went high on every side, just having everyone home was satisfying.

The days had been fun as they enjoyed their time together. The togetherness brought memories back in abundance.

Things really seemed to be getting better. Jesse prepared to return back to his house and back to work, but not before he promised his family that he would not disappear again as he once did.

Jesse left from their view as he went into the departure lounge. It was at that very moment, that John sensed a moment of peace rest within his heart, as if the blocks that were once thrown down, were finally being re-built since Dad's death.

Nothing seemed to be right since then, well not until this moment.

John and his mother headed back home, knowing his mother would be a pleased to get some rest after such a lovely Christmas.

Well the fun was over, and mom was doing much better, and things were back to normal all over again. Only this time, mom was not working as hard as before and John felt a bit more relaxed since things were getting better.

Not only was work back to normal for his mother, but John took work to the racist old man, with little regard for what he might have said.

Professor Stevens, looked at his work that was so pristinely done with amazement and mumbled that his work had potential, but he could see in his eyes the envy he felt over a mere student who had come up with this revolutionary idea instead of him.

John smiled a bit on the inside, knowing that no matter the case, he was still going to publish it. Every week after that, he was researching more on the idea, as well as finding as many experts as possible who would be willing after due consideration to authenticate his idea and who would see to it he got his work patented and published so that it could be of help to humankind.

John cared little for the recognition and fame that came with publishing works of that nature. He was more concerned with the value of the work that his children, if he ever actually had any, could benefit from.

It would not be the first time that he would have this thought; neither would he try to blank it from his mind. He made up his mind that the perpetuating thoughts would better be dealt with by confronting them directly.

One day, John got up after his classes and he went down to the cemetery. It was the very same one that his father was buried in. It would be the first time in ten years that he went to look for his father's grave, and it would be the moment of truth, where he would lay his attachment to it and find the closure he needed in his heart. He looked at the white painted tombstone, with its black lettering on the front.

It read, "A father, husband and a man of integrity." He stood there reading it repetitively, as if to suggest, reading it again would somehow put to rest the trouble in his heart. He did as many before him, in times past. He began to express how he was feeling, how his heart hurt from his sudden departure; and for a brief moment a tear came to his eye, and for once he allowed himself to feel the brutal nature that is emotions.

Every ounce of turbulence within his mind evaporated into thin air, as he finally accepted the peace of closure and the relief of expression.

Soon enough, he got his works of discovery published. He was working on it for so long that finally ushering in his achievement, he realised that it was his final year in college; and the days had passed like a summer breeze through the trees.

It was amazing that once the past is properly laid to rest in the cemetery of closure, new life can sprout from its resting place.

John looked for Tim, on the day that he got his book published, and truly Tim was his best friend, for he shared in John's excitement as if it was his own.

Tim's eyes widened with disbelief, as the grin rose from one side of his face to the other. He walked forward as they collided in a bro hug. "I am so proud of you. There are little words to express my exhilaration."

John accepted his words as if it were coming from a brother from the same womb, and with elation they went out for a bite, as they went over to the most loved fast food restaurant in the city.

They served the best hamburgers which were mouthwatering decadent. The culmination of sweet and spicy, intermingled with a rich bàrbecue sauce that was deeply marinated into the meat gave it a scrumptious taste that was to die for.

Whenever there was something big to celebrate John and Tim would go there to eat, it was like a tradition in their friendship, and so it remained.

They would be going out more frequently as the weeks followed. John made sure that amidst his success, school was still a prime priority.

Even Professor Stevens, though not as happy from John as he was himself, didn't fuss, and started treating him more fairly in classes; which propelled his ability all the more, for there was not a class that he did not excel in and it was known throughout the university.

CHAPTER 11: GRADUATION

It finally came time to graduate from University, and mother was back to normal. Jesse decided that he would call more regularly, and Tim found himself a girlfriend as they prepared to step into a new chapter of their lives.

John had no doubt that something happened the day that he had gotten closure at his dad's grave.

He couldn't explain it but it was almost magical, as if the years of burdens that were laying on his shoulders were gone, and now he could walk freely. He was happier than before, and he knew it.

This new feeling which spurred in him like a freshly discovered spring gave way to a flurry of confidence that prompted new ideas and aspirations; and it wasn't long before he started looking for a new job.

He had made it through school, with all its difficulties, problems and hardships, and with everything he had the rejoicing spirit of gratefulness, exuberating satisfaction and a calm sense of humility grounded his emotions

Over the past few months, while trying to finish his studies, he would move from job to job desperately trying to obtain a john which would best suit his skills and his intelligence level, as he figured that this would better enable him for the future.

About three weeks prior, he had obtained a job in the law firm just about three miles away in the city. It was well-paying job that made ample use of his intelligence.

The goal of finishing school with no debt seemed to be on the horizon, as the sounds of his feet began to click along the sidewalk, the rushing of a vehicle sounded through the air.

Tim was really working hard as well, trying to maintain his grades as well as look out for his best friend. Sometimes he would just make a copy of the notes for John if he found that John may be late or that he might not come to class and John accepted it gladly.

They fought through tiring nights of studies through the years and battled many sorrows. From the death of John's dad, to the illness of his mother, and being mistreated in school because of the colour of his skin; it would be much for anyone, but thankfully, they survived it together.
Tim knew that John had the new position and he went to visit him from time to time. Today was no different.

He would arrive at the grey, white and black painted building of a law firm, press the buzzer at the door to signal his arrival. John always looked happy to see his best friend, but today was different, there was a thick darkness in the air.

John looked at Tim's face and could see the dismal expression of grief or sadness exuded from his demeanour and it caused him to instantly question him to figure out the cause.

"Tim!" John blurted out with a surprise, knowing that he had never seen Tim this low before. "Man what's wrong with you?" He questioned.

With a sour expression on his face and an almost emotionless tone of voice, void of any feeling he responded "Someone stole my car. The thing is that I am not even mad, because it was a dumb car anyway.

John remembered the car like yesterday, well that was the last time he did see it, but he thought about the first time he got the car. They went to the museum to celebrate, and then they drove over to the science convention fair, the movies, the park, and the library.

John remembered his first kiss that he got in the car from Helen, who had been a gorgeous blond haired young lady, with the glowing skin tone of someone who tanned her skin well. More than her looks though he remembered the conversations that they had, which evoked smiles and grins as each spoke to each other.

They had been getting close for some time, but that was before hearing that she would no longer be around since her parents accepted jobs in another city and that meant that they would move away.

It was after this John's focus shifted from any one woman to his ambitions. He made up his mind that he wouldn't allow anyone else in his life who may leave, so he kept to himself from then. All the memories that the car had, came back.

He looked at Tim dead in the eye as he placed one hand on his shoulder and gave him words of solace which any good friend would. "I'll help you find it."

After working in the firm for a little while, he became familiar with many of the law enforcement agencies that were around, and he would now use that information to his benefit.

John grabbed the phone at his work place, and his face expressed such focus and intent that it scared Tim. Looking in a small black book with red trim along the edges, John began calling different names and numbers to intervene in the situation.

It wasn't long after, a man with a fresh and crisply ironed

suit walked in. The suit was jet black, and he wore a white dress shirt with a red tie underneath. His stature was tall and slender, and his face stout blank and expressionless. When he walked in there was nothing said, just a look between John and him as if to suggest that there was no need for words.

The silence was unmistakeable as Tim looked over by John to suggest that he needed to speak to him, John looked at the man and at that moment, the only words that were uttered were the ones used as he asked to be excused.

Tim followed him, he asked what was happening as he could not understand exactly what had just happened.

While Jesse had been there, he had given him that very same black book in case anything was to happen. John now took the opportunity to seek some help that he otherwise might never have needed.

When they re-entered the room where they left the man, he was seated with his legged crossed and a certain readiness on his face that was distinguished from just a normal blank face.

John nodded at the man, and it was at that very moment, he got up and gave John a card. He told him to call the number that was on it, in exactly two days at that very time.

When he left, everything seemed to have gone back in motion as normal. Tim still feeling uncomfortable, just tried his best to ignore his uneasiness, but as the hours went by he couldn't help but wonder, who the man was and what it is that he was doing.

It was this that gave him such bewilderment.

Two days later, John followed the directions that he had gotten from the man, and when he called him he was welcomed with pleasantries which gave way to the reality of what he had done what he had left unsaid.

After, the casual greeting, he heard him say, look outside as he heard the click from the phone being hung up.

John's heartrate began to increase as he didn't even get a proper response, but he did as instructed and to his amazement, the vehicle was there and parked neatly in the driveway.

John, walked outside to the car and on the seat was a letter with his name written in big and bold letterings on the envelope. It wasn't until then, he found himself truly understanding the extent that this man would have gone.

Within the envelope was a picture of the man, and a note indicating that he was to burn that letter and its contents, before 4:00 pm.

John looked down at his black watch, and to his amazement it was almost 4:00 pm. His gut instinct insisted that he go and burn it and so he did.

At exactly 4:00 pm on the dot a call came in and it was the man on the other end. He had called to ensure that John had truly discarded in the letter as was instructed. Failure to do so would have activated a tracker and signalled a group of men to come to the location of that device and execute specific unmentionable actions.

After explaining that it was a test, John's fear was realised as he was just beginning to understand the kind of people that he was dealing with. He would never forget it; but with the vehicle in the driveway he was somewhat relaxed, yet he could not help but wonder what happened to the man in the picture.

He shook the thoughts out of his mind and grabbed the keys as he carried it to Tim who had decided to stay over with John for a couple of days.

John looked at time and said "Open your hand" as he dropped the keys of the vehicle, which held memories of his once forgotten love. Tim graciously thanked John and ventured out the door as he journeyed to his place of abode.

Since his mother's illness John had been staying home more often, but today he wanted some fresh air and to walk for a bit. He went upstairs as he took up his blue hoodie which bore the Ohio University's logo, and a pair of black khaki pants and a pair of sneakers.

Walking out the door, he could tell that he made a wise choice with the hoodie, because the atmosphere held the presence of a chill that would grow colder throughout the evening hours.

Only being about 5pm in the afternoon, he could still see neighbouring citizens casually walking up and down, all seemed to be mentally preoccupied with their own problems to notice anyone.

There were children who had been playing hopscotch on the side of the road, their chanting brought back recollections of his childhood days. The singing moved from hopscotch, which seemed to be over when he passed, and transferred over to jump rope skipping.

It was a good deal to see these youths, play and be outside for a change. As things changed over the years from just ten years ago, he noticed that many of the children his age didn't want to play outside, and how could he blame them, with the ground covering in blood, or other body excrements which probably came from a fight the previous night. Many times there would be needles that would be left behind close to an alley way which suggested the habits of the drug abusers around.

John, would have complained, but he knew of the predicament that surrounded his neighbourhood, and his side of the city; which is why he hated the idea of failing. Failing meant that it would be harder to get out of this God forsaken place, and that meant more to him that he fully understood.

John just continued walking as he heard some footsteps coming behind him; but because of his lack of fear for his own area where he grew up he paid no attention to it and he had good reason. This was his home, and even though he hated it, he knew everyone and everyone knew him. Even if he didn't know them personally, they certainly would know his father and his reputation in the area.

He looked so much like his father that the person that walked up to him, had not noticed that it was John and assumed maybe it was his brother.

Upon reaching him and seeing his face, they blurted out

"John, it's you" to which John replied with a generic answer to just close the conversation. Walking away, his mind went back to his surrounding as he saw the cat that he feed months ago, looking as mangy and scrawny as before.

He didn't walk with anything that it might eat and for a brief moment he expressed his sympathy before he resumed his journey to nowhere. He eventually found some friends that he decided to hang out with, which was a nice way to spend some time.

It had been about two hours after his walk that he decided that he would go home, so that he could see about getting some schoolwork done. This would be the final paper that he would need to submit before walking up the aisles to his own graduation song.

He hustled home to get his work started and for 4 hours non-stop he worked on that paper. His drive kicked in as he wrote and edited repeatedly, to ensure that every line and every ounce of information was both scholarly accurate and editorially perfect.

When he finally completed the paper he was drained, as the expression of satisfaction spread across his face like butter over a slice of bread which had been just freshly cut from hot bread out of the over. His grin went from ear to ear as he contemplated his completion as well as how much closer he was to actually getting to his dream of getting out of the slums.

CHAPTER 12: PHOENIX

After John submitted his paper, he realised he had more time to work and save his money. He decided that he would take time out to do things that he would find more enjoyable, like his habit of enhancing his memory capacity and knowledge basis, which meant reading a lot.

John decided that he would seek every university that he could amidst everything that he was doing. Everything seemed to be going too well, and for a brief moment, he contemplated what could have brought such an ominous feeling in the air; suddenly he heard the rustling sounds of leaves being stepped on, and the hairs on the back of his neck stood up.

There was no other person around, and he couldn't figure out what it was. The sound began getting louder and seemingly closer to the building, but just then as he looked out the window; he saw it was just a cat playing in the leaves. It was a false alarm.

He was so tired and his eyes burned as he rubbed them. It was nice to be able to go and get some shut eye, and that he did, but before falling asleep, he went to check on mom since they tried to converse more with each other since the hospital incident.

He spoke with his mother until it was 1:00 a.m. which left

them both really tired. He looked over at her and wished her a good night and told her he loved he dearly, and she responded with a hug, and said "I know, I raised a good son. I love you too"

They parted to their individual beds, and while mother went to bed and fell asleep immediately, John laid in his bed thinking about life and his future even though he was dreadfully tired.

He made up his mind that for the next six months he would look to broaden his horizon, so as to provide a way to make himself and his mother more comfortable, and with his eyes closed shut he could feel the contentment of his plans being fulfilled in his imagination as he drifted off to dreamland.

The night erupted into dreams, while he tossed and turned in his sleep, deeply entrenched in the subconscious imagery that played in his mind like a movie, he accidentally walked into.

He could see a beautiful eagle, with a glistening white shine that gleamed off of its feathers from the sun in his dream. It flew so close to the sun that its large body came to the centre of the sky, blocking out its light.

Like a phoenix it spread its wings across the sky just as John opened his eyes. He knew what it meant. It was him, he was about to soar. With his mind settled, every day for six months he worked harder than anyone else in the law firm and he realised that his desire to become a lawyer grew like a ball of leavened dough, as his passion like sugar fed his ambitions.

After four months of nonstop work, his efforts were noticed by the man who was working with him; who rewarded his with more and more sensitive projects.

John slowly, rose through the hierarchy of the corporate system and within a short space of time John had double, nearly tripled the efforts that would be needed to get him to rise above the status he so desperately desired. Leaving work at strange hours in the evening from the office, he was no different from his mother who would work tirelessly to provide.

It wasn't long until his potential was also noticed by a beautiful woman, with light brown hazel eyes, and athletic body structure, which provided a high aesthetic appeal.

She walked into the office one day, and could observe the intensity of focus exuding from this young man. He had not noticed her presence, neither her intensely piercing eyes which seemed to be fixated upon him. It wasn't until his search for a particular file to complete one of his projects that his gaze turned in her direction and he noticed her glare.

He immediately noticed her appeal, as her purple dress fitted itself upon her with an exquisite curvature that complemented her curves and features.

John tried his best to keep his eyes off of her as he without a thought, initially ignore her stare and continued working. She left after about 10 minutes, and for the time that she was there he couldn't get her out of his mind.

It was as if she set a spell upon him, because it wasn't long before he started seeking information about this woman. He knew she had to have come in there before, and he went to receptionist to find out if they might know who she was.

To his disappointment, he couldn't get any information on her, but he needn't have worried. A week later she showed up again, but this time she looked at him for a brief moment, and went to speak to the director.

After she left, he went to him to ask who she could be, trying desperately to make it seem as professionally inquisitive as possible. John noticed that his director, Mr Brown with his clean shaven face and brown skin, looked strangely similar to the lady; John could not help but think that they may be siblings.

To his amazement, Mr Brown showed a small grin on his face as he which was barely noticeable, as he confirmed that it had been his sister. It was the first time, in a very long time that he was interested in anyone and it scared him.

John finished his work, and went home as usual, but this time he chose to go visit Mr Jenkins, who was still a major mentor to him; he changed his course of habit to ask him for advice.

John was barely at his house for more than five minutes, before Jenkins walked out with a smile on his face as if he had now seen the lost prodigal son. It had been almost six months since they had seen each other.

He looked at John as he walked to him and noticed how much his features had changed in that short space of time. Not only had John grown a little more, but he also had begun growing a beard that was well groomed.

As he walked to him, he felt for a moment as if it were his very own son who had come to see him; and it brought a smile to his face.

When they finally reached on the porch to sit and talk, Mr Jenkins asked if he wanted anything to drink and he went to get the drinks. Mr Jenkins had a typical porch that came with white boards, rocking chairs and netted doors.

The house had been around longer than John had been alive, he could tell from the creaking noises that came from the floor boards. When Mr Jenkins finally returned, John began asking him how he had been, to which he responded by explaining that things were getting better but he needed to be more careful.

After a few minutes of general conversation, and jokes; John began to ask questions on relationships, and how to handle it.

It was at that moment, that Mr Jenkins's wisdom which came with many years of experience had presented itself with accuracy.

John listened intently as his lack of experience was now being filled with the expertise to handle himself as a young man, which would potentially gain him a partner for life.

One question that John asked which stuck a cord in Mr Jenkins was, if he knew so much why he was not in a relationship. He turned to him and responded "John, I was married for twenty-seven years and my wife passed away, eight years ago. It was just her time."

His face sulked for a moment and in his southern accent he continued his statement "whatever the reasoning, God knows best. That don't mean I don't miss the fine gal, she was a pretty little thing, but for now all I can finds time to do is reflect and help young men like you."

John felt a level of appreciation overcome him; he had been working so hard, he almost forgot to keep tabs on the people who have always been there for him.

To think it had almost been a year since he was doing his degree, and though he wasn't doing anything close to his science degree, he found himself liking his new career choice, and he was learning fast.

John looked at Mr Jenkins who did not look even a day older since their last discussion in the hospital, and it caused a smile to form on his face. His dimples made him an attractive person.

The two sat there discussing relationships and need of gaining a companion for almost two hours, and both John and Mr Jenkins could not even tell that so many moments had slipped away into the river of time.

It was always an experience coming to see him, whether it was on the bus or at his home, he was the same Mr Jenkins he had known.

It wasn't too long before the sun began heading to descend over the horizon that John looked at his watch and noticed that it was 6:00 pm.

With an almost sudden halt to the conversation that they were having, John respectfully excused himself as he got up and headed for the door.

They wished each other well wishes as he walked out the door, but before he left Mr Jenkins with a calmness that comes about from age, asked John to return when he had the time.

They were like father and son, and it was always a pleasure when they both got together to sit and talk. John looked at him as he stood in the marble coloured hallway of his front door, which looked like mahogany, and agreed that he surely would come back.

He left to try to get some rest for a new day, and to maybe do some research on a project that he had started, but it wasn't much longer after getting home, that he heard the sound of gunshot ricocheting through the air. It seemed to be about fifty yards away which was kind of close, but John had grown accustomed to those over his years of life; from time to time they would ring through the air like fireworks in the night. He was sure it was nothing and John went to bed.

As he lay in bed, he heard a knock at his door about an hour later. Someone pounded the door heavily, as if it was a policeman, and to his surprise it was. He was Tim's father, who was a retired policeman. He wasn't a very tall man, and from the way he spoke you could tell he was a slick man in his days. He had a cool jazz tone to his voice.
He wore a well pressed soft pants, and a dress shirt with the sleeve rolled up, but on the ends of the shirt there was blood.

John looked at him with shock, wondering where the blood came from. Tim's father looked at him with sadness that you could feel, the kind that made the air so thick it was hard to take a breath. With a chocked response he said, "Tim's dead."

There was dense silence for a few seconds, and before John could respond, feel or do anything. Tim's father went back to his car leaving John in shock as to what just happened.

John couldn't feel anything, it was too sudden. He finally came to himself, and walked upstairs to his bed; tossing back and forth, he got no more than three hours sleep that night.

CHAPTER 13:TIME TO LEAVE

John woke with a strange yet familiar urge to leave. It had never been so intense before. It was as if he was incapable of refraining himself from succumbing to this urgency towards leaving.

John took all that he had with him, well at least everything that could fit in his suitcase. He packed with an almost carelessness towards what may happen next, and even amidst his packing every thought of what could possibly go wrong flooded his busy mind.

John heard his mother walk through the door of the house. He had already packed by this time and he grabbed everything to carry them downstairs.

He picked up a nearby blue inked pen and searched the house for a piece of paper as he scribbled down that he was leaving for a while. He had deliberately left the time frame vague, so as not to give her undue anxiety towards his return.

Finally, he rose, as he took up his bags to leave the house. He left to find something, something that he could not find if he stayed.

His departure was so sudden, that it shocked him to realise

that he was capable of doing something like that. He didn't know what got over him. He kept thinking over and over about what he was doing - like moth to a flame he continued to his path.

John disappeared for a two years without any trace. It was as if he was lost, and no one could find him, not even he himself.

It was months since anyone heard from him, and his mother longed for him every day. Her last born was out there, somewhere and she couldn't see him or know where he was.

Every day, she missed him.

What wasn't known to her was that the John she knew and loved would not be the same man that would return. John had done so much in his short time away, that it seemed almost un-believable.
He went to Washington in search of where he could use his skills, which were his heightened intelligence and thirst for knowledge. He definitely was not the average black man, and he certainly showed that in everything that he set his hands to do.
Rising in the ranks of socio-economical stratifications made him feel a sense of pride as his plans flourished like the blossoming of a flower into the cascading colours as the sun paints the morning sky.

John had not allowed himself to properly mourn since Tim's death; It was so sudden. Too sudden. He found out a month later after leaving the true reason that Tim had been shot. Though they were best friends, it seemed that Tim had a hidden life apart from his ambitious ways in school.

Tim had been doing business with a nefarious character, so that he too could alter his situation financially. This man told him that he seemed to have the skills necessary to partner in a business venture with him.
The man proposed that he would do the production of the

drugs, and all Tim would have to do was just capitalise on certain projections of sales around various neighbourhoods and his success would be assured.

John could hardly believe that he would do such a thing. Thinking about it he could hear his own voice in his mind saying, "how could you do something so stupid man? Why didn't you tell me?"

He felt a warm tear escape the corner of his eye. The salt water drop rolled down his cheek. John lifted his hand to his face as he wiped away the tear.

He could do nothing else but reminisce on the good times that they had. The guy limes, and even the days of study, where they would venture into the river of knowledge as they tested each other, so as to ensure that they were always ahead of the rest.

It was funny how, life can abruptly end. That at any moment, anything could happen; it was right at that moment John evoked a decision within himself since he could die at any point whether it was his fault or not. John decided that he would enjoy every moment of life that he was allowed.

Falling into a state of rebellion to his own feelings and even his own conscience, he began his walk the descent of the bottomless pit.

Knowingly and unknowingly, he had subjected himself to a new way of thinking, one that would cost him, much more than his time or money. It was this attitude towards life that would give him, both his most inspiring moments that would take his breath away, and adversely the ones that would send anyone into the abyss.

The journey continued with a new perspective, one moment he was the apex of his endeavours with a lust for life and success that outshone the world, the next he was all that his world could offer, with its good and bad.

CHAPTER 14: BEGINNING TO THE END

One morning, he woke up and everything had changed.

He looked in the mirror and realized that his face had started to mature with the time that had presented itself upon his appearance. For a moment, he mourned the loss of his own reality.

His mother had not seen him since he left those years ago, and he couldn't find it in himself to go and see the place that reminded him of not only his father's death, but now his best friend's.

While looking in the mirror, he blinked for a moment before he felt his body hit the floor. He blacked out for a moment as another dizzy spell came over him. It certainly was not the first for the past year. It had been growing frequently and with greater intensity. At first he assumed it was all the late nights that he spent working as he built his career.

Over the last few years he completed a law degree, and he was rising the corporate ladder, much quicker than any of his counterparts because of his determination and stellar work ethic.

His dreams of coming out of the "hood" had come to pass. Though he never saw his mother since the moment he left; with his steady rise to influence and power, he had more than enough to provide her with the comforts that he thought she needed, and he never hesitated to ensure that she was financially secure.

He had reached his goal, and it seemed like a noble victory, but there was something about finally reaching where he wanted that seemed almost dissatisfying, and he could feel it in his stomach; it was in fact a hallow victory that he could not shake.

It took him ten years to establish his efforts into reality and by this time, he was thirty. He had not only completed a law degree, he had gained his masters, completed over one thousand cases on trial before he reached his present status, and he had achieved the number one spot as the most sought after defence attorney.

His position afforded him the same money as though he did all those cases simultaneously. Now he handled two to five cases the most per annum, him and his team. There certainly were many overnighters just to ensure that the cases were handled not just well, but excellently.

Although his life seemed to be going according to plan, of late his health had been deteriorating; and with it came his constant voyages to the doctors.

Finally, it happened. This time when John had awoken, he found himself in the hospital. It was the very first time that he had ever been hospitalised and, for a slight moment he felt a sense of shame. Not a shame from being in the hospital but rather that he ended up in a predicament that would be negative to his reputation.

His anguish of being there was a bit worrying. John signalled to a nearby nurse who was in the same room attending to an elderly gentleman who seemed to be suffering from some sort of shock.

He beckoned the nurse to his bed, but she continued to attend to the gentleman.   When she finally finished assisting the man, she spoke with John, who questioned her on why he was there and how he got there; and with a motherly tone that came from those that are versed in medicine, she answered and explained that he had fallen ill and had blacked out whilst getting ready for work.

He knew in his heart that it would have been only a matter of time, before the sickness that was raging in him would prey upon him.

Even now as he lay in bed he was a man free to acquire everything that he wanted, he had the means to go wherever he desired, but yet like the fate of all humankind, he was stuck in his own prison, holding on to the hope of release from the penitentiary of his own sickness.

It took the doctor four hours to finally come and attend to John, and to give him a thorough explanation as to what had happened. The moment the doctor began elaborating on his condition, he realised that this had been something that didn't originate recently, but rather it was something that had been festering within him for years, and had gotten progressively worse.

The doctor told him that in fact he did not have very long to live. The sounds of impending death, seemed to be imminent at the door of his life.

A sense of utter hopelessness flooded his emotions as he questioned vehemently as to the prediction of when he may meet his inevitable end.

The doctor looked at him directly in the eyes and with a slight pause before he expressed his verdict, he answered that John would have approximately one year before he would die.

John's heart began to beat tremendously, as the ECG showed the rise in his heart rate. The sounds of the slow rhythmic fluctuations began to exaggerate into a flurry of chaos.

He tried to calm himself down at the sound of the news which upset him. The doctor as well as the nurse tried to assist in calming him down. It took them ten minutes to pacify the reaction and the possible effect that it may have on John and his now recognised illness.

John had developed Leukemic cancer and it was severely widespread. John had contracted not only one form of cancer but he had three other forms of cancer as well. No one could have expected this to happen, especially John.

John stayed in the hospital for a few more hours before they discharged him and let him go home. Upon his departure, he called for one of his drivers to come and pick him up and take him home.

There were no family members, no loved one to come into his life to make it any better, but rather it was just him and the success that he had accomplished. He had done nothing in the past ten years, but work. His social life was very little and lacked vigour.

He went on the occasional travel, but even that would be something relating to work.

On his drive home, he rolled the window down as he allowed the breeze to flow over his skin. It was the first time in ten years that he had taken the time to appreciate the simple pleasures of just feeling the breeze on his skin and allowing the tingling sensations to remind him of the joy of existence.

The sight of a child playing in their yard, a dog playing catch with its owner, all seemed so new, and invigorating while he looked out the window with a new interest. Simple pleasures of life, like the taste of one's favourite dessert after a meal, came to him with urgency, as he contemplated his life thus far and the shorter life he had left.

John got home after a twenty-minute drive, and with his mind scanning the recesses of his own thoughts, they began to seat themselves upon his chest.

With a level of urgency, he opened the door to his open concept apartment which had all the latest titanium appliances that would make any home glamorous and sleek.

The rug was of a fluffy texture, and felt like the pelt of a freshly brushed horse mane.

The kitchen had a large island with a lovely marble top and a black and white back splash which gave an aesthetic appeal that would make anyone want to live in such a home. His home was completely detailed to a man who was destined to be single. He rarely ever contemplated getting into a relationship, because he viewed it as a distraction from his goals; but now as he stepped into his home, he noticed a stillness that had never affected him before.

There seemed to be a newer recognition of his present state of mind, as he came to acceptance that his life could potentially end much sooner than he imagined.

John decided to take a shower.
When he finally got out of the shower he put on some fresh clothing as he intended to go out. He wore long khaki pants, and a plain white shirt with the sleeves rolled up. He headed out to his black and red Porsche, which he bought only a year ago.

John wasn't one to dress overly fancy, he believed in a level of simplicity that should speak to his personality. This became his reality since he would not let himself be dominated by the general thinking when it came to possessions and money.

He required money not because he wanted to appear to be something to anyone; it was never for the appearance, but rather to leave the world from which he originated. It was his biggest fear to be poor, but now with a new reality of things, a new fear conjured itself, and it was the fear of never having done anything with his life and never making an impact.

He drove for what seemed like hours without ever stopping or coming out of the car, and his mind raced as to try to figure out what he could do to overcome the illness. His tenacious spirit would not allow him to give up without a fight and that was what also propelled him to start to invest in his past, so there could be a better future; then it suddenly hit him, he never made the effort to return to his old home and to see his family. He never tried to start a family, never to make a difference that could be long lasting and it drove him to truly reconsider all that he had done up until that point.

CHAPTER 15:DEATH ROW

J ohn had driven to the point that his eyes were collapsing on themselves. His eyes began to blur as he looked out the windshield, as his eyes began to shut he heard the sound of a horn blaring from a fourteen wheeler, rushing towards him.

His heart was racing when he finally grabbed the wheel and pulled to the side of the road with a sudden urgency. Not only was his prediction of death inevitable, he almost quickened the inescapable.

His heart pounded so loudly that he could hear the beating in his ears. He was panting with heavy breathes as he held his chest with his trembling hand.

What was happening to him, how so many things could have escalated so quickly, from his dad to his best friend, his mother? Now he was sick and he only had a year to live.

He pondered on what he could do in a year and all the things he could try to get done before all had come to its final stop. The only thing that was on his mind now, was getting home. He knew that if he didn't that he would be sleeping in the car, and the thought of that shook him awake.

He had turned off the engine when he pulled over, but turning the engine back into life, he revved the accelerator, as he looked for landmarks to signal where he had ended up.

To his amazement, he recognised a where he was, it was actually not very far from where he went when he first got to Washington.

There were stores which were completely engulfed in darkness as their vacant appearance signalled their lack of human existence.

With his trajectory set, he set off for home, which took him only an hour to get back to. He passed many lights on the way home and the empty streets, like a ghost town from its once busy isles and alleyways.

The street was still busy as though there was no sleep for those commuting to and from, but the walkways were barren and lacking human interaction and busybodies.

There seemed to be a similarity with the street at this time of the night and the value he felt in his life. He had provided for his mother and became what he set out to be, but what had he done to impact the future generation, to better the world somehow?

The question was left silent in his mind for a while, and it wasn't very long before he would come to realisation as to what he could do.

John reached home and settled himself to bed, with the exhaustion that overcame him, his slumber was almost instant-aneous when his face had hit the soft white pillow; in a matter of seconds John was out cold for the night.

When he awoke to the sound of his screaming alarm clock, he got up with a fire in his stomach that propelled his step to an even greater aspiration. When he set off to work that day, he had about ten more days of work to do, to complete a case that he had been working on for the last 3 months, everything was going in his favour; the many nights paid off.

John challenged himself for the next ten days, as he worked tirelessly and without fail. When he had come to the completion of this final case, he informed his immediate superior of the diag-nosis that he had gotten eleven days prior. In light of his con-dition he informed his superiors that he would be withdrawing from the company as a result of some needed time to re-evaluate life.

In the beginning the answer seemed to be swaying in a direction which would be counter-intuitive to the answer he sought, but after providing some legal documentation and evidence of his condition, it was only fair that his request for time to be granted without a push from corporate heads. He made connections with many firms and men of status and power, and with this benefit he used every bit of it to his advantage.

Just as he had stepped out onto the busy roadside, he could hear the chitter chatter of many people walking casually past and the sounds of a busy street as the cars drove by; at that moment, just like when he was standing in front of the mirror, he felt his body weight shift almost as if he were floating in the air, that was the initial feeling before the collapse.

He laid there on the pavement as his head spun with the speed of a spinning top. He had on a suit that cost almost five thousand dollars, but in that moment, the only thing that he could care about was life or death.

A small cluster of people came to aid his plummet, and to ensure that he was okay, but their humanity seemed weak, until a young lady came his way. She wore a white dress with golden edges that made it seem more appealing to the eyes.

Her sparkling hazel eyes were mesmerizing, as her fair beauty caught the attention of all those who passed by. It would not be the first time that he would see this woman, and it would be this woman who would come to assist him, more than anyone else.

While he lay there a million thoughts came to mind, even Tim was on his mind, and how he wondered if his inevitable destiny had come sooner than expected. He had so many things planned. He realised he didn't have a family of his own, and he may never own the company he was so tirelessly working to climb the social ladder.

Just the same as water fell from the sky without the hope of rising again, so too were his dreams seemingly crashed against the tide; but like the rain, for it to rise again, it had to change form to elevate to its once forgotten home, and the sky is where they roamed.

John found himself blacked out once more, as the ambulance transported him to the hospital. He regained his ability to recognise his surroundings after about an hour.

He scanned the room and to his amazement, he saw the beautiful woman, and it was strange because he got a sense that he knew who she was, and it stumped him. Without thinking clearly, he blurted out, "do I know you?" "I don't think you do; but I know you." She responded with a soft voice, which complemented her appearance immensely.

But John did know her, and it was not the first time that he saw her. She looked at him, with such endearment, that he was sure that he knew her.

She could see the wheels turning in his mind as he tried desperately to figure out who it is that he was speaking with, and it gave her much pleasure to see his confusion. She had always enjoyed his peculiar ways and drive, and she would enjoy every ounce of his momentary confusion; as it would be only a matter of time before the intellectual John Carter figured out who he was conversing with.

She did not spend longer than was necessary and with that she took her leave without another word. John propped himself up on the bed with his pillow as he stared in silence, watching her leave. He wondered who she was and it bothered him, that for once his confusion was of his own accord.

He felt like he should know who it was, but there were more important things he thought that were on his plate, and that certainly was the case. His prolific mind was compounding ideas on top of one another, and figuring out who this random woman was, was not a priority for him.

The dusk of the day came with the canvas of the sky painted with its evening colours to signal its coming darkness. But with the night gaining momentum, John's mind though filled with a barrage of thoughts, he could not eradicate the desire that he had to know who this woman was, and why she came to assist him.

Trying to reason in his mind whether or not he had the time to make the mystery known, he leaned to the crystal of ignorance. With a call for the nurse, he probed her with numerous questions of the state of his health, but as if trained to not say anything, she redirected the question to the physician who was to come to his aid.

Frustration grew wildly along his face as the wrinkles from the years of hard work folded over each other, as his expression of calmness collapsed into seriousness. She looked at him and understood that he had every right to be frustrated, but though she was not giving the information, it was out of not being privileged to the knowledge of his condition. That was why she did not respond the way he thought she needed to.

He could see the panic on her face, as if he did not see this a million times before and it was at this time that he realised that she knew nothing about the case.

It was the typical facial expressions of a person who was trying to pass time or was trying to make up something well enough to pass the interrogations. His thousands of hours of lawyering and getting information had come in handy yet again.

He wanted to comment crudely concerning her ignorance, but he held back his blatant words that would cause her even more emotional distress, and with a calm deep breath he slowly released the air from his chest as his lung deflated and his chest collapsed slowly down to invite new air into his nostrils.

After, he simply told her it is fine as A type personality began being triggered by the feeling that his time was being wasted.

Getting up off of the bed, he held on to the IV hanger and rolled it along with him as he went in search of the doctor.

The nurse desperately tried to insist that he returned to his bed, and to his surprise they had changed his clothing and given him a bed gown; but with his tenacious ways he continued to his present goal.

As he approached, the doctor with startled eyes called for another nurse so that they could get him to return to his bed, but he refrained once again, as he said in a voice so stern that everyone stopped what they were doing, "DO NOT TOUCH ME!", then dropping his voice, he spoke calmly, I demand to know what is happening to me.

The doctor realised that there would be no reasoning with him until he got the answer he was looking for. With a relaxed voice, he asked "May we return to your room, and discuss this properly?" John retorted quickly, "Finally, that is all I asked for, some information. I don't have all day, and neither do I have all year. I cannot afford to waste another minute."

They walked back to the room that he was in as John returned to his bed, and the doctor to a seat which was nearby. Pulling it closer to John, he asked John to sit on the bed rather than lay.

John knew tactics like this well, especially when bargaining with criminals to get the confession or to get victims to hear what you would have to say.

"John, there is no way nicer to say this, than to tell you the truth. I'm sorry to say that you don't have much more time to live."

John blurted out, "When are you going to tell me something I don't know? What I need to know is how much time do I have left and what are my treatment options?"

"Because of the advanced stage of your cancers, and their spread, I am afraid that even chemo therapy will only make it worse for you. "

John knew that he may not see the life that he wished but, hearing it once again caused his heart to sink. He had done so little, experienced so little and for what, to never be able to enjoy the fruits of his labour?

With a grieved heart, he looked at the doctor in his eyes with his glasses glaring the light from the fixture above, "How much time do I have?"

"Mr Carter, I say that you have about nine months to live, before the cancers completely take over your body, and puts you into a state of shock that will cause you excruciating pain."

John had expected to feel maybe some rage, or sadness, maybe even a hint of psychosis, but in that moment as he realised his time was growing shorter, he felt nothing.

It was as if all emotional reactions seemed so obsolete that his brain filtered it through to air. Like the sweat coming out of his pores, his emotions filtered through to the side of nothingness.

As the conversation reached an end, the doctor gave his remarks of sympathy to John and walked away with the nurse to give him time to think through everything that he would be dealing with.

John called back the nurse quickly. The thought of his life going out without a fight was not a thought he could live with. When the nursed returned to his bed side, he asked for a few pieces of paper and pen. She looked confused for a split second, but she too from her years of experience, knew too well of the grieving process and coming to grips with death.

Many had different methods, some cried tremendously, some suffered shock and numbness, some went into a frenzy, some began to regret times past, and then there were the "Johns"; The one who would formulate a plan to make it better, to do something with the little time that they had.

These people were always the ones who came across as the most eager and excited about trying everything, sometimes to their own demise; but she assisted his request.

She left the room and returned with a few blank sheets of paper from the nearest printer, and brought a black inked pen to write with.

He thanked her with the blankest face, and as she left John immediately began writing things he had never done. Up until that time he had not truly allowed love into his heart.

From experiences of not exploring life to travelling more, he wrote it all, but at the end of the list, the last thing that he wrote was returning home to see his mother.

It dawned on him that he really had neglected communication with his family, but what he did allow for was financial delegating.

With his mind fixed, he started from the bottom of his list upwards. He picked up his phone which was placed on a table next to his bedside, and scrolling through his contact list he spotted his mother's number, which he refrained from calling, as if to say that she would evoke emotions that he did not want to deal with maturely at the time, but "fate" had now dealt him a hand of cards that only he could choose to play with carefully.

The beeping of the numbers on the screen of his phone, created a sensation in him which seemed to be fear. He observed his body and the state of his mind as all digits were pressed, and staring at it his heart raced as if he were running from something terrifying, his mind went into a negative overdrive, thinking if it was the right thing to whether she would be home and while he observed his thoughts, one question popped into the consciousness of his own reality.

Where did this fear come from? Are babies born afraid of things? Are dogs born hatting cats? Then when did this begin?

The philosophical thoughts blossomed in his mind, like a budding flower to the rays of the sun on a spring morning. "It is not real fear, but rather the subjection to ones' own belief of something."

He breathed heavily as he pressed the call button on the phone, that button that seemed to have gotten larger the moment he pressed it and the very same one that seemed to reflect ending the call begged to be pressed, but he refrained as he could hear the ringing tone on the line.

An older woman answered the phone, she sounded vaguely similar to his mother. The voice was much older. "Hello he answered, I am sorry I think I have the wrong number."

"John is that you?"

He instantly realised even his mother's voice has grown over the years of separation.

"Yes mother I am right here. How have you been?"

With the sound of tears in her voice, she answered, "my son it has been very long. I am very happy to hear from you."

His heart broke to hear her after twelve years from being home, two when he drifted in the limbo of coming to himself, and the other ten years of nonstop work. He noticed that though he had been sending money religiously, it wasn't enough to satisfy the yearning in her heart towards him.

A single tear came out of his left eye as he felt the warm wet droplet run down his cheek, he had not shed a tear for years and there had been hidden wounds that needed healing and though he released his pain from going to visit his father's grave, he had not yet buried the death of best friend in the grave of his mind. Like a seed that became a tree, its burial only seemed to grow into permanency.

With strength that he had to muster from inside, he replied as he ensured that he took a deep breath, I think that I am coming home. He knew that he couldn't bring himself to telling her about his condition; it was too soon.

His mother could hear that he was hiding something in his voice, she listened intently to him as he expressed his desire to come back home; but whatever the reason, she was happy to know that he would be back.

Click, was the sound of the phone hanging up as the conversation ended.

This would be the very first solution to the problem he faced. Knowing that he had not gotten over his past, within his mind he did not want to leave the world without first cleaning his past of any undue hurt that could have been caused to him or to anyone else.

CHAPTER 16:GOING HOME

Finally, they let him out of the hospital, and as he stepped out he pulled the suitcase that had his clothing behind him. The young lady that constantly kept returning to check in on him while he was there came to his mind. He had finally asked her, who she was out of the sheer curiosity of it. She wouldn't tell him until she came to see him she said, and today he was being released from his so-called prison. Fortunately, she left her number, but was without a name, where she advised him to call her. He took that offer, and called her to assist him in getting back home where he could relax before his soon departure.

When she pulled up in front of the hospital, she saw him in a plain white t-shirt, plain soft pants which were complemented by some well-fitting sandals; and the titanium watch adequately gave the appearance of calm wealth. John knew how to dress, he was never flashy and the only thing that he would splurge on was his watch collection.

His identity was not in his ability to make money he always thought, but rather in his ability to work. He knew too well of the symbiotic relationship that came as a result of diligent work and success, money was then the by-product of these two elements and he strived for their continued cooperation.

Stepping into the silver car, with its luxury seat, he was

calmly surprised, but not shocked at her vehicle. It was an Audi vehicle, but one for the upper echelon, and it fitted her well.

She looked over at him and couldn't help but internally admire him. They made light conversation, before John grew impatient to the mystery that burned in his mind. "Look let's stop playing games, you have been coming to see me for the last two weeks, and I need to know what it is you want, and who you are?"

She knew well that this was the John she knew when they were younger, he was fiercely straight forward. A small smile perked at the corner of her face, as if to signify that she got what she came for.

"You may not recall who I am because we have not seen each other since I left, but John it is me."

Like a sudden epiphany he peered at her gorgeous face, filled with the maturity of graceful aging, and it instantaneously dawned on him, that he was looking at the one woman whom he had loved in the car that was stolen those many years ago.

His past flashed through his mind like a blazing rocket. It was Helen and he had not seen her since they were sixteen years old, and now they were staring at each other once again. His priceless dumbfounded expression made her grin all the more, I knew you would not be able to remember since our last days together.

There were so many questions, and it seemed that faith had brought them back together. Helen had become one an excellent business woman, even going as far as having established a successful skincare line, which aided in youth retention, which explained her beauty enhanced by glowing skin.

She didn't have blond hair anymore, which didn't make it any easier to identify who she was, her hair was dyed jet black, and it flowed down the sides of her shoulders like silk.

John was less interested in her looks at this point; he wanted more to figure out how she came in time for when he would have fainted. "What were you doing at the office front when I was leaving?" John questioned to appease his curiosity.

Helen pulled off the side of the road and looked John directly in his eyes with a piercing gaze that felt like she were staring into the depths of his soul. "John if you have not noticed, you need me right now, and as it stands I don't see how that is important right now.

He looked back at her with equal intensity, and he felt something that he had not felt in a long time, and for a second his mind quieted and he could feel the world around him. It was as though for that split second, everything connected and it revealed itself.

"You came for me, didn't you?"
She knew too well that she could not lie to him. It was as if he could see through her, and she loved him for that. "John I came to check in on you when the news came out that one of the top lawyers in the best firm was leaving, I came to see you."

John looked at her wondering, why if she knew where he was, why she didn't make an appearance before?
Seeing his thinking face was appealing to him, and she adored his expressions.

Then suddenly it dawned on him, it was the new press which released his withdrawal from the company that gave her his whereabouts.

"You figured it out because of the publicity that came with my retractions from the firm?" John asked
"You're always too smart for your own good. Yes, John if you must know."

He knew it and he didn't seem too bothered by it all, deep inside he was glad to see her again even though he didn't verbally say it, and neither did his face, but his body spoke to his unspoken words.

Helen pulled the car from the curb as she took him home to get out of the city. When he finally got home it was 12 o'clock in the afternoon, and as she left for the rest of the day, he thought of their conversation, but more than this the reality was still prevalent at his door to his imminent death and he needed to leave. Within the space of two hours John had fully organised everything for his departure to see his mother.

Little did she know of his arrival, and the suddenness of it. John went to bed early that night; for the first time in a very long time. When he rose at 4am it would take him approximately three hours to get her house.

     The cab pulled up in front of his once forgotten neighbourhood, which had not changed much. He still saw the addicts forging through the trash bins in search of materials to assist their unhealthy habits, like starving dogs looking for their next meal. The spray painted buildings still showed their violated bodies, as one whose body had been molested by the hands of paint

     He loathed this place, the thought of coming back sent shutters down his spine, he had bought another house for his mother about three years ago, but knew that she wouldn't want to part with this house

     Out of all the houses hers looked the best, since he made sure to have it maintained and supplied. It had recently gotten a new coat of paint and the lawn was cut to the perfect length, which gave it the appearance of elegance as you basked at its presence.

     The house was much better than he expected as he walked along the brick walkway that he ordered to be installed a few months ago. It had solar power circular lights planted in the earth next to the walkway, which assisted in preventing anyone from falling at night.

     John grabbed his entire luggage as he walked up to his mother's front door. She could hear the sounds of the engine outside as the vehicle parked in front. She pulled across the curtain and for a few moments could not recognise him, until her eyes adjusted to see properly. When she realised it was him, she hustled to the front door and swung it open as she stood there gazing at her last born.

     His face had changed, and he looked more like his father than ever before. His matured face had started to develop winkle lines, and very small amounts of grey peaked through the forages of his beard; but when he walked up to his mother and hugged her she recalled the warm embraces that she once got from him growing up.

Memories flooded her mind as she held her little boy, and feelings of pride and happiness overwhelmed her as she thought about what he became; but before she could utter a word, she felt the warm tears escape her eyes as she continued holding him, and though she missed him immensely, she could not help but enjoy the time that was now present with her son.

What she did not know was that he would only have a few months to live and this would be the beginning of the last moments she would have to remember him.

John realised that she had sobbed on his chest as she hugged him tightly, when she looked up, he could see the mix of happiness intermingled with the sadness that exuded from her face.

"Mom", he spoke softly as he looked at her intensely, almost feeling ever movement of emotions that lingered between them, but unlike her, his knowledge was grounded outside of the realm of her ignorance of his reality and it broke him internally to know that these may be the last moments he would have with her.

Life, it was like a sneeze, it moved with rapid intensity to slowed exhaustion until all were gone into the nothing of where it once came.

He fished in his mind for the right words, but none came as he simply held his mother by the shoulder, but none came to mind, and it was as though no words were needed, in the silence of the night. She signalled with her hands that she wanted to get him inside the house.

It didn't take long for the air to filled with laughter and chatter from the two of them. They had not seen each other for many years and it seemed that it all that was once a mystery now bursted out into surprise as well as sadness.

After their initial conversation John thought it best to leave the most horrid news to another time. As the conversations slowly became halted by the sounds and sights of dropping eyes and yawning mouths, they closed off the evening as they departed to each other's room.

When John entered his room, he seemed to be almost taken aback when expecting a messy room which may need a bit of a cleaning, was spotlessly maintained. Even the bed was made up with what looked like fresh linen.

It was almost as if, his mother knew he was coming and adequately prepared for his arrival. There was no fuss neither a complaint when he came, but he was welcomed with open arms, and for a second as he placed his bags on the floor, he felt a deep pain within his heart, but he could not allow the emotions once again to overwhelm him.

He decided to walk through the house, and as he did so, a million memories came suddenly to his mind. He recalled the time Jesse had thrown him into the wall; a small chuckle came to his face as he thought about the time he placed a live ant nest in his bed for when he went to sleep.

But as he walked through the living room, there was the picture of his dad, him and Jesse. This was before he left. "Good times" he thought as he headed but up the stairs.

John looked around the room and saw the picture of his brother on the back of the door, but when he turned to the wall next to the window, he recognised the picture of his best friend and himself as they stood next to each other posing for the camera. You could see it was an old picture, John had his hand over Tim's shoulder and Jesse had on his awful red sweater which looked like he was walking around as a strawberry all day long.

He pulled the picture down as a smile cracked along his lips as he looked over the picture once more. It was funny how life threw him so many curve balls, but with every throw, it seemed he was given the swing to connect.

Working hard was essential and he could not display a spirit of lackadaisicalness in his pursuit, otherwise it would bring him to his own demise.

He really thought it best for the sake of the family, to work so tirelessly, and it seemed that he was correct. Until, he started feeling a tingling feeling in his lungs as though he wanted to cough. It seemed minor, but the sensation intensified tremendously, and in a matter of minutes John was coughing profusely.

As he coughed he rushed to the bathroom as phlegm coated the inside of his throat but he let out a glob of mucus into the toilet bowl, he was shocked to the sight of blood coming from his mouth as it intermingled with all that had spud from his insides.

In that moment, the reality of his finality came to his cognition, and in a moment of panic and fear he felt his heart drop to despair.

His hand reached up to grab his chest as if to hold his heart, and with his shirt in his hands, he pulled himself up from the bowl, and went over to the sink. He washed his mouth out, but and stared into the mirror, wondering a thousand thoughts.

Why? Was the very first one, and he couldn't figure it out anymore and he stopped trying. With the quality of life receding rapidly like the hairline of an old man, creeping to its soon extinction, he too felt as though his life were about to come to a sudden closure; one that he was not sure if he were ready to face, not yet at least.

John flushed the bloody mess down into the sewers, hoping to pretend that he did not just catch a glimpse of his own mortality. All the years of undying work and diligence, seemed futile and vapid as the wind now that he may never get the chance to enjoy it.

He took a deep breath, and exhaled heavily as if there were a weight resting on his chest. When he went back to bed, he found it impossible to fall back to sleep, and tossed and turned all night.

His mind flashed through thoughts of his father, and how

much he wished he at least got to see him grow, he wished that his brother didn't leave so early, he didn't leave his mother for so long. With his mind racing all evening he realised that he had little time to do everything that he wanted to do and he had to find every opportunity or create it to enjoy the beauties of the little life that he had left.

It was about 4am, when he came to the sudden realisation that he could do anything for the next couple months. He wasn't tied to his desk, and he was condemned to any meetings, but this time he could enjoy the experiences of the things he never found the time to.

Within minutes, John got up with a ferocious drive towards living. It was his way of saying that he cannot and could not go out without a fight. He had gone through too much, to give up so easily now, and he determined that this disease would not beat him.

John, pulled out his laptop, and within a few minutes he had sent emails out to every head of directors to start a foundation, with investors to create a project fund to assist his neighbourhood.

He called in favours from all over as he expressed his desire towards the project that he now had. By 9:30am, he had gotten seventy-five per cent of the responses he was looking for.

He didn't expect to get everyone on board, but he did get a few investors and directors willing to accompany him in managing it; this would ensure that upon his inevitable departure, would not be faced with legal allegation and would not be subject to any unnecessary hurdles that could induce any failure of its ultimate success.

A smile crossed his face as he realised that the first step was already accomplished, and it raised his morale instantaneously. His white teeth shun as he walked out to his mother who was in the hallway, sipping a cup of raspberry and sage tea.

Looking up at her handsome son, she could see a glistening glimmer in his eyes, but before he could even say a word, she asked him one question, "I haven't seen you soon in ten years, where have you been and who are you?"

She looked at him intensely as if to inflict his conscious mind with a guilt that was impressing upon her own heart. She felt as though her heart was about to erupt as she looked at her long lost boy.

John walked to his mother, with his towering height; he pulled her close as if he felt every emotion that raged through her mind. As he embraced her he could fell the water drops flowing from her eyes as his shirt began to be drenched by her tears.

John was not the type to express with tears, but as he held her, the emotions which had been welled under his subconscious self, released, and the feelings of warm liquid escaped his eyes as drops of tears flowed down his face and into his mother's hair.

There was a silence in the air as they stood there. Only the sounds of cars passing outside could be heard.

John loved his mother and she loved him, and this was one moment that he would cherish for as long as he lived.

Though John enjoyed the moment of love and empathetic mutuality, he came with a goal in mind and he determined in his mind that before he left this world that there would be an impact.

John had called around a few favours, and they were coming together finally. For the entire day, he had meeting after the meeting, getting all the legal documentation to start his first project. His first official project would be to ensure that a college fund was set up, and it would be a recurring annual event, which would give youths of the neighbourhood a fair chance to attend school and advance themselves.

This was only his first project which he assigned all of his focus towards accomplishing. John stayed by his mother for four weeks, while he handled all of the running around. At every moment he took the opportunity to spend time with her, and he made sure at least once a week they went to dinner.

There was one person who seemed more interested than him was Helen. She had called to ensure that everything was going along well, and with genuine concern in her voice asked about his health.

John's health had been deteriorating, and it was become more pronounced upon his face than before. Even his mother started to take noticed after the first two weeks, but he was adamant to be a good trooper and not try to cause any distress during this time.

Meanwhile, John did everything to ensure the success of his plans, but there was a bit of a setback, one of the investors had withdrew from the project and that left the $50,000 short of the budget needed to start the foundation.

When John got the bad news, he called every firm, corporation and company, and whoever he had past dealings with and, it wasn't until a week later that he got a response from a CEO of VisionPlex, one of the leading providers for eye care, came to his rescue on the account of a favour that he owed John.

His brother had been absent for all the actions that was taking place, and with prominent position, things seemed to be doing well on his side. This is where John would ruin his streak of things that couldn't go wrong.

John took up the phone, to call his brother. He heard the husky voice that he was accustomed to hearing, but instead of greeting him with fine news he called to tell him of his condition and asked him to be there for him as soon as possible. During the time that John was doing everything to resolve the project's hiccups, he also had took the time to see some of the most qualified doctors around and to get further assistance on his method of fighting.

When he went, the doctors informed him that he would need to treatment immediately, if there was even a hope of getting over his cancer. He felt as though that were a win in the direction of maybe being able to fight back, but at the end of their conversations, each doctor told him the same thing. With the level of spread that he had contracted, it would take a miracle for him to live, and that he would only have about eight months to live.

Jesse, after listening to everything that he had to say, only could reply "this isn't over."

There was a click at the other end, as he hung up on John. John was a bit confused but he understood Jesse more than he realised, and he let it good. He didn't try to question it or even call back, he knew Jesse needed time to think and deal with the situation.

When he had gotten back by his mother's house, he let her in on the good news of the success of his endeavours, and he could see she was proud of him. It would be the first major thing that he did for the community.

Within days, he was once again all over the news press. "Lawyer starts a "Fund the Youths" to local city." John wasn't impressed by the media, he was only doing it to help his community, and to give back to where he once resided.

It wasn't long before the impression of the illness struck once more. He found himself once again in the hospital, but his mother was there, to comfort him, as he held her hands.

It would be then that she would find about his condition and her heart broke to know she might lose the son she just got back. While he laid in the hospital bed, he smiled at her, with the energy that he could muster. And he could see a glimmer of a smile spread across her face.

He spoke softly due to the little energy that he had and said with a faint voice "I want you to know I love you."

They spoke for hours while she sat by his bedside. They expressed every thought, and emotions that could be felt.

All the unspoken words began to flow between them and the most honest conversation about everything emerged. Events which took place at home, all the mischievous things they did, it made light of the atmospheres. There were jokes that were told which lit the air with laughter, and though John's expressions were weak, they were genuine and carefree, as were his mother's.

Many things were spoken, and it reunited a bond which had been burning low. When John was released, they went home, with spirits that were once down and saddened, but were now lifted.

CHAPTER 17:FINAL PROJECT

John and his mother began making plans on the new project that would start to improve the poverty stricken community.

The tide seemed to be changing for both them and the soon to be updated community. It was merely a matter of time before the plans which were conjectured to improve upon the dilapidated neighbourhood, would arouse the blossoming eloquence of new life.

The depths of depravity and despair, as it were in John's eyes; was nothing more than a formidable foe which he could utilise to propel his determined spirit to fight against.

He had garnered assistance from all over the country, ranging from national agencies, local bodies, as well as regional government assistance. Within a matter of days, there would be the beginnings of a new play park development, which would enable the youths to have better play facilities. Clubs to keep the youths active was also implemented within the advertisements; some of these clubs were of athletic affiliations, some were for educational purposes which would enable those to take on a new skill, whether it was computer science, or merely learning how to sew. There were also wide spread talks of the new developments, which included publicity that promoted the advantages that came with the place. One thing that John hated the most while he grew up there was the drug related problem which stemmed from various causes, and he wanted to do something about it.

One of the ideas that he wanted to try to assist with, is a drug reform and restructure program. This would entail the drug addicted fiends on the street would be taken to a facility which could help those who couldn't make the change on their own, while being able to supply them with jobs and keeping weekly progression reports on those who left for up to six months so as to ensure that the change was long lasting and that there would be few if any relapses.

John had barely begun to implement the program, before he faced his first set back. A few of the members on the Board of directors who were reviewing the project proposal, began to question whether or not the plan would be effective in creating the change that he described.

In the end, John came back not only with a few of the same board members, but also supporters who were influential in the upper echelons to present their opinion on the matter.

Fortunately for John the meeting when finally adjourned brought an unanimity amongst the board members which created a cohesion towards the completion of the plan.

With his forward thinking mind, the skillsets from each member on the board, the willingness and the community ready for a change, there would be nothing else to stop him in his tracks.

Over the next three weeks, John worked along tirelessly with the various bodies and was happy to see the defaced buildings gaining a facelift which for him was invigorating. Although it was merely in a small region at the time it would soon reach the major sites. Just the beginning stages alone brought a sense of morale and boosted the spirits of those who were witnesses to the newly organised improvements from a local.

Though John was firstly ashamed of his origins, he learned to embrace it with full assurance that in the face of adversity and uncertainty anything can grow. The idea that acceptance of one's beginning does not equate to the reality at one's end came to his collection of thoughts.

He was not sure that he was willing to give up his fight for life either. It was a Tuesday afternoon at 3:00 pm that John had gotten the contact information of over three dozen highly qualified doctors to inspect his case.

Each one told him a variation of the same thing he always heard, his life was shortly to be captured by the hands of death. Little was offered in terms of treatment and the little it that was offered would only give him an additional two months.

When he had looked at all the time spent on the project thus far, John had barely six months to live. With one phone call to his brother, he decided that he would find every excuse to do everything before he passed.

John picked up the phone and called Jesse, using his private number. He needed to get on to him urgently. When Jesse answered the phone, he heard the tiredness in his brother's husky voice that only a brother who grew up with his sibling would be able to pick up on.

"Hey Jesse its John I need to talk to you, it is an urgent matter, do you have the time to talk?" John asked. "Mom, told me already, I will be home in two weeks." "Alright, I will be waiting. See you soon." Click

The phone was hung up and John could sense that there was something off, but he could not put his finger on it. With little time to spare, he also called up Helen who was more than happy to come and meet him.

She had been there with him through so much and though he could not understand it, he knew that she must have loved him to fore bare the strain. Whatever the case was, he appreciated her and a sense of connection began to form as the moments rolled by. When she showed up her hair was gracefully done, as she wore a summer's dress which accentuated every curve of her form.

For a brief moment, John could feel a smile spread across the outline of his lips, which compelled him forward as he looked at her. Her eyes locked with his, and in a moment the daze of suspense climaxed into silence.

Nothing was said, but every unspoken word was heard, and it brought calm to the atmosphere. The silence was deafening when Helen spoke only three words, "I love you"

She knew fully the impossibility of his recovery, and though she had prior knowledge to his horrendous end, her heart was linked to something that may only last until Christmas.

When John heard those words, his heart raced, he could hear its beating as the sound of the hooves of horses as they ran on the racetrack. The escalation of his breathing caused him to take a seat, as Helen walked over to his side. Though he had not realised it, he had developed those feelings also, and in trying to suppress them he found them intensifying.

Sensing his discomfort, Helen suggested that they go out for some fresh air, and with that they ventured out for a drive. The local park had been halfway finished since the last time she was there and he wanted to show her the progress that was made.

When they got to the park they could see the beauty of flowers, arrayed all across the lawn, and the half-finished play set. He drove though the areas that had been refurbished, and many of the dilapidated building defaced by graffiti were repainted and remodelled; the bricks given new life as they breathed the air of aesthetic appeal.

The neighbourhood began baring some semblance of pride once again. It had been over 50 years since the last time, members of the community would call their beaten down city a place that would bring pleasure to the minds of both outsiders and those living there.

John felt a sense of contentment as he looked on all the work he put in and it pleased his heart to know that he accomplished something for his neighbourhood.

John face had an expression of elation as she looked over and could not help but be overwhelmed with happiness for the man she had loved since youth.

John could feel her eyes looking in his direction, and as he gazed back with an intensity that seemed to slow time, they leaned forward towards one another as their breaths shortened and as their faced pulled closer in romantic embrace, his phone went off obnoxiously and in that moment the magic was lost.

John answered; it was one of the investors on the line, who had called to inform him that the plans he had to open the funding program, had been successful with the government board. Within a short space of time, he had accomplished much more than many had not even attempted to do for the once defeated city.

The organisation's main location was situated in the heart of the city as to give accessibility to the residents living both far and near. From the moment the final legal documents were signed to open for business, little by little people from all over, started to inquire and apply to be granted the aid to better themselves.

John decided that he would inquire as to how it was that they settled the legal side of things so quickly. When he called and began asking questions it was reported to him that because of his credentials and their associations, they were able to navigate through the negotiations of the terms and conditions with the government and legal officials in a much shorter time.

John knew exactly what that meant; they pulled some strings. He understood the white collar game well. He once played it better than most.

His mind drifted again to his brother, and he wondered what he was doing; he had not forgotten what almost happened between him and Helen, but he tried to keep things simple, knowing that he did not want her gaining an attachment, which would cause her to be heartbroken if he died.

They continued speaking as they drove back to his home. Emotions lingered high in the air. Nothing was said about what happened, It was as though it never happened.

When they arrived back the house, they walked in the house to express the good news. John saw his brother there with the very same doctor who had initially told him that he had about nine months to live.

What John didn't know was while he was out making changes to a community which had given up on itself, Jesse was out examining every piece of documentation and medical records that had gone through various doctor's hands over the years that John had begun searching for means to a solution.

When John had looked in the eyes of his brother, he could not understand why they were there; but as he asked the simple question of the purpose of their presence, he noticed within the hand of the doctor was a white envelope with a red mark on the top.

Jesse walked over with his muscular stature and large shoulders and stretched out his hand to collect it. He looked at John who's faced looked more and more confused as every second passed. "What's going on? And why is he here?" John asked with a troubled voice.

"I need you to read this, and read it out loud." Jesse replied as he handed the envelope to his brother.

The letter read:

Dear John Carter,

It has come to our attention, that there were some inconsistencies on the previous diagnosis of your condition. Your condition is in fact a rare disorder that mimics leukaemia and is extremely exacerbated by stress. This condition however, is not terminal.

We fully expect your symptoms to lessen with time and some much needed adjustments to your lifestyle.

We deeply regret the pain and anxieties caused and wish for you a long and fulfilling life.

Regards
Doctor Jude Brown

It took merely a matter of seconds, before a tear ran down his check as emotions flooded his mind, he dropped into the sofa, sinking into the cushions.

It was almost too much, almost more than he could handle. Not only had John done something incredible for the people who lived around him, but in that moment he was with the very people he loved, everything was alright and would be for a very long time.

www.ingramcontent.com/pod-product-compliance
Lightning Source LLC
Chambersburg PA
CBHW072053150726
47999CB00005B/1758